Marilene Habersetzer
at Frances on the Willapa
74 Strozyk Rd.
Raymond, WA 98577

6-8-16

THE HELIANX PROPOSITION
Or:
The Return of the Rainbow Serpent

Timothy R. Wyllie

Trade Hardcover Edition ISBN 978-1-935187-08-0

Gift Edition (w/Slipcase) ISBN 978-1-935187-09-7

Ebook Edition   ISBN 978-1-935187-11-0

The typeface in the main text, Lizard Script, is designed by the author.
Author photo: Robert Drexel, and photoshopped by Kesara
Anderson Printing House Pvt Ltd, Kolkata-India

2012

Daynal Institute Press
www.press.daynal.org

For
D.K.W.
and
the Cosmic Seed
in all of us.

The Helianx Proposition
is appearing in a number of different formats.
This includes a collectable handmade, archival, limited edition
as well as a more broadly published art book.
Giclée printed archival prints of individual pages are also available.

Acknowledgements

I would like to thank the following people for their support and encouragement over the years it took to create this work. Foremost, my deepest appreciation goes to *Diana Wyllie* for the means and the freedom to follow the dictates of my heart. To the women in my life in the course of this long 25 years goes my ongoing gratitude for their patience with my curious obsession; *Damien Henriques, Hilda Brown, P.R.D'or, Alma Daniel, Carolina Ely, Elli Bambridge, Urszula Bolimowska and Anna Moore.*

I have kept this project very private so that only a few of my close friends have been aware of it. Amongst those who knew and encouraged me along the way are *Robert Faust, Scott Taylor, June Atkin, Kevin Sanders, Robin Desjardins, Andrew Tatarsky, Ruth Strassberg, Flame Schon, Rob Drexel, Nikola Wittmer, Nina Reznick, Nathan Guc, David Field, Kathe McCaffrey, Byron Belistos, Genesis P-Orridge, Lady Jaye Brewer P-Orridge, Armand DiMele, Gabriel King, Rachel Garcia, Glenda Lum, Carlos Avey, Elianne Obadia, Andrew Ramer, William Giese, Edward Mason, Michael & Cornelia Eckett, Yanni Posnakoff, Mark Howell, Peter Russell, and Christopher Castle.* A special appreciation to my friend of over 40 years, *Malachi McCormick,* himself a maker of exquisitely crafted hand-made books, for his encouragement and always humorous advice over the years.

My thanks, too, goes to *Fredric Lehrman,* who heard The Helianx Proposition related many years ago and who has maintained solid support to this day. He was also kind enough to write the brief opening statement included in this edition.

I would not have been able to finish this project without the constant advice and expertise of *Miqui Mendes* and *Ernie McIntyre,* of SouthWest by Miqui. Acknowledged to be the finest Giclée printer in the business, *Miqui* has gone far beyond any expectation with her loving care and deep expertise. This book would not exist in its present form without her technical advice and artistic brilliance.

To *Robert Davis,* who magically appeared at exactly the right time and whose enthusiasm and support has made the final stages of publication possible.

Finally, I'd like to thank my friend, *Daniel Mator,* whose consistent interest and intelligence contributed invaluably to the final edit of the Commentary.

The Helianx Proposition is a cosmic fable, a creation myth that floated down to me late one night in 1979 in an unbroken six-hour stretch of writing. I'd been meditating on the deeper symbolic meaning of the traditional Christian Garden of Eden scene and wondering, yet again, whatever the Serpent was doing there. Since the creature's impact on the two humans in the story was apparently so profound, it raises the issue that the Serpent, too, had a transcendent origin and a valuable function to perform. Perhaps under the veneer of Christian blame, there lay another, very different, story. With that thought, The Helianx Proposition started writing itself.

I invariably pay more attention when a piece of writing comes through in an easy, steady flow, seemingly descending from elsewhere, fully thought-through and needing almost no editing. And The Helianx Proposition certainly caught my attention. So much so that I decided to spend however long it took to calligraph and illustrate the story, starting off by using graphite on parchment. In my mind I had planned to do each page in color, but I didn't feel confident enough in my medium of choice and hoped that future computer technology would have developed to a point at which I could apply color to the drawings.

By 2001, the technology had arrived in an affordable form and I started to have the black and white pages digitally photographed and then printed on watercolor paper, using a high-end ink jet technique called Giclée printing. I then set out to learn Adobe Photoshop with the idea of using their software to color the images. I soon realized it would take me even more time to color the images digitally than to do it by hand, and not half as much fun. My color sense had developed over the intervening years so I chose to add color to the printed images using Prismacolor pencils and various dry pigments, re-photograph the page, and then clean it up and make any minor adjustments using Adobe Photoshop, before finally printing it.

Original graphite image   Computer enhanced   Completed hand-colored

I was fortunate to find some references concerning the Helianx buried in the 2034 edition of the Codex Galactica. I have included many of these details in the Commentary that you'll see on the opposing, left-hand pages. Much of the Commentary was received while I was in the mild-trance state I require when I'm drawing and was written considerably later than The Helianx Proposition. I have also included a Helianthropic Glossary at the back of the book for the broad definitions of the words and terms italicized in the Commentary.

Because of the fluid and seamless way in which The Helianx Proposition came through originally, I believe there may be elements of great interest to those who sense there is more to life on this planet than meets the eye, and which will, perhaps, add some insight into the odd persistence of the presence of Dragons, Nagas, Plumed Serpents, Cosmic Snakes and Rainbow Serpents in the stories we have told ourselves over the thousands of years of human history.

Timothy Wyllie New Mexico 2008

Contemporary readers accustomed to narratives featuring the terrestrial, extra-terrestrial, and celestial functioning as one in the dramas of cosmic evolution may enjoy musing a bit upon the word 'Helianx'. It resembles closely the word 'Heliand' that was used for the word 'Savior' in what may be the only surviving poetic work of the Old Saxons from the 9th century. That the same poet likely composed as well a more lyrical rendition of the creation story from Genesis as a companion piece offers some historic framework for better exploring the transformative possibilities suggested by this alternative creation myth by Timothy Wyllie.

While some early reviewers have found in this narrative a reminder of William Blake, as this edition of The Helianx Proposition was being prepared, the work of Carl Jung known as The Red Book, suppressed for over a century, was finally released for publication. After examining Jung's work, it appeared obvious that a closer kinship may have been found here given the use of finely calligraphed text and stunning visual art to explore the sometimes frightening images of the unconscious occupying the mind of one of Western civilization's pioneers of the inner life. Indeed, the promise of The Helianx Proposition may well prove that what Carl Jung accomplished in his long suppressed "Red Book", successfully transforming the personal demons of his inner life into avenues of liberation, Timothy Wyllie does with comparable artistry for Earth's troubled memory, probing the meme of ancestral loss to find the truth of an 'original blessing'- the real treasure we are.

Robert L. Davis, Daynal Institute, 2010

INTRODUCTION
by
Fredric Lehrman

"Many aeons ago, as measured by our present way of calculating time,
there dwelt in the vast, dark, velvet curve of Space…
a band of enchanted Space Gypsies."

Thus began my first hearing of the Helianx tale. These trance-inducing words were spoken in magical, deep, slow British tones in a darkened room before a large glowing fireplace. The voice began without preamble, and the speaker, silhouetted before the embers, his long white hair shadowing his face, seemed no less than Merlin himself.

The circle of listeners in the great salon that night in 1983 included writers, Nobel laureates, film directors, brain scientists, publishers, business leaders, psychologists, actors, research chemists, several teenagers, and a few urban shamans. It was Saturday night of the first "Mad Scientists and Artists Party," a three-day gathering convened by social visionary Marilyn Ferguson at a friend's estate south of San Francisco.

The important things in life grow in value through reflection over time. The aural transmission received by the rapt audience that evening has had its own ripple effect. The story matured in the minds of both the listeners and of the teller of the tale, Timothy Wyllie, and now, in its evolved form, it comes to you as this book.

I had first been introduced to Timothy by Marilyn Ferguson at one of Buckminster Fuller's last lectures in New York. She brought us together saying, "You two are both interested in dragons." In the space of the ten-minute intermission, we reveled in being able to plunge right in without having to justify or explain ourselves. We both already knew that something was afoot if a "myth" is accompanied by similar descriptive imagery in cultures on all continents throughout known history. If dragons were "imaginary," why then did everyone seem to 'imagine' them as large phylogenic hybrids, part snake, part bird, with claws like lions, manes like horses, and voices like thunder, or some other improbable and colorful mix? The Rainbow Serpent of the Australian Aboriginal, the feathered and dazzling Quetzalcoatl of the Aztecs, the benevolent bringers of wind and rain of the Chinese, or the fierce and feared abductors of maidens and hoarders of treasure of Northern Europe — dragons were everywhere.

"Dragons are often held to have major spiritual significance in various religions and cultures around the world. In many Asian cultures dragons were, and in some cultures still are, revered as representative of the primal forces of nature, religion and the universe. They are associated with wisdom—often said to be wiser than humans—and longevity. They are commonly said to possess some form of magic or other supernatural power, and are often associated with wells, rain, and rivers. In some cultures, they are also said to be capable of human speech." -— From Wikipedia, the free encyclopedia

To pursue such mysteries is to "ride between the worlds," as the Celtic storytellers are apt to say. The book in your hands is your ticket to that ride. Here are some suggestions as to how to assimilate what you will see and hear.

You might start by reading the Text aloud to yourself the first time through. It will taste different that way. Find yourself a quiet spot with good acoustics. (The Queen's chamber in the Great Pyramid of Gizeh comes to mind.)

In its present form, The Helianx Proposition unifies three stages of expression. The original story can be read in the calligraphic Text, later illuminated by the images that emerged over nearly three decades of intuitive work. On your second reading of the Text, slow down even more and let the written words resonate with the dream forms and colors.

Eventually, when you feel that you know the tale well and have soaked awhile in its pool, start to add the third and final layer of the text on the facing pages. As with many ancient philosophical manuscripts, an original text is revisited by later scholars, who then write commentaries to assist the student in deriving more from the information. This is something like what Timothy himself experienced while working on the book during the thirty years since he first wrote down the story.

In the facing-page commentaries you will be offered additional details, and be asked to consider new concepts and be invited to explore vast spaces. You may find yourself going carefully, gradually deciphering and integrating new terms and levels of interpretation. Little by little, your mind's eye will broaden to take in vistas of cosmic dimension, pulses of time so long as to be beyond the awareness of any less long-lived than the Helianx.

This suggested way of reading recapitulates my own journey into the primordial world of the Helianx, that great antecedent to our more recent notions of the dragon in all its forms. The interplay of the three levels of information presented in this book resembles a kind of exponential Bach fugue, with themes moving at different speeds and weaving themselves together in inter-dimensional flows of time.

At some point some of you may begin to recognize yourself in this music. We all have capacities yet untapped. We are able to sense the possibility of the Helianx practice of group telepathy, feel the genetic cargo of the ancient archives of Helianx memory, and connect with the task which Nöé embraced, to pass on the precious dormant seed of that vast encoded experience to the worlds of the future, eventually to be brought home to the waiting community of minds.

The flower that opens then will answer the great question…

"Why?"

Fredric Lehrman Seattle 2009

THE HELIANX PROPOSITION

OR

THE RETURN
OF THE RAINBOW SERPENT

The Helianx are believed to be one of the few still existing species to have been created on a planet in the second of the seven vast *Superuniverses* that together comprise the *Multiverse*. Since the superuniverses are said to be formed and seeded with life sequentially--and we currently inhabit the seventh--this suggests that the Helianx are the most ancient race of intelligent beings yet encountered. It should also be remembered that movement between these seven superuniverses is all but unknown. It was the general presumption of this extreme unlikelyhood that has allowed the Helianx to keep their presence in the seventh superuniverse a secret for so long.

The use of the phrase "technologically proficient" in the text needs to be understood in a very specific sense when describing the Helianx, since almost all their technology was the result of the direct control they had over their own biology. Think of them as the original gene-splicers--except they preferred to do it internally. Using their proficiency at *quantum bioengineering,* they were able to assemble organic *nanobots* that cruised the veins of their massive bodies, cleansing, repairing and ending up by rendering them virtually immortal.

Amongst the more practical applications of this biological manipulation was the ability to create tools as physical appendages of their limbs. This could be a time-taking affair; with the nanobots working directly on the individual's *messenger RNA* building a functional implement, cell by cell, which would allow a Helianx to interact more fully with hir environment. With these tools, and the skillful use that they were able to make of modulated sound waves, the Helianx were able to craft their magnificent underwater world.

The original evolutionary impulse on the Helianx planet of origin was in many ways very simple, but also very different from the techniques used in the development of intelligent life in later eras of Multiverse organization. The approach used was known to be very reliable, but unlike planets on which a wide variety of creatures predated on one another, it was also exceptionally slow. After the successful *seeding* of the life plasm on the planet, a process of molecular aggregation was triggered that led to the formation of cooperating cells. Over time, these contributed to the structure of rudimentary underwater vegetation and then, after many millions of years, to simple aquatic creatures.

Through further cellular aggregation, and countless small acts of *mutual symbiosis,* a species eventually emerged that was a fusion--a single species comprised of many different collaborating life-forms. Evolution then appeared to focus all its attention on this one species and over the course of its history individual beings went through an astonishing array of different physical forms as their size increased and their ecological space opened up. It has been suggested that some of the properties of *DNA,* created as the basic organic code linking all life in the seven superuniverses, can be seen most clearly delineated in the persistently helical metaphysical structure of the Helianx.

A continuing challenge that faces a description of the Helianx is one that confronts any commentary on a telepathic species: that of psychic boundaries. Where does the psychic influence of one individual Helianx cease and another one start? Is it really possible to speak of an individual Helianx as separate from the collective? How can an individual Helianx ever be considered as different from any other individual Helianx in a fully telepathic society?

Once upon a time, many aeons ago, there existed in the velvet curve of space an enchanted race of space-faring gypsies. They were an old and wise race and cunning in their own way, too. Now cosmic travelers, they had arisen in much the same way as any technologically proficient species, their DNA codes trudging them through unicellular boredom,

out from the soft wetness of the pan-universal ooze. Unicellular became multi-cellular... micro-molecules became macro-molecules... the millennia passed...

There has been some disagreement among academic *Psychomystics* as to whether the biological control the Helianx had over their bodies could be considered true shape-shifting. But all concur that the ability must have stemmed from their point of origination in the second of the vast superuniverses. Although very little is known of that era, it can be assumed that matter, at that point of creation, was more fluid, more malleable, and much more easily subject to the control of a powerful mind. When the Helianx were the sovereigns of their underwater world, they communicated with one another not only through a type of *bio-acoustic telepathy,* but also by skillfully modifying their bodies both in form and hue. In that way, they believed every nuance of a projected thought could be shaded by a constantly shifting spectrum of color.

Similar in principle to the Earth's plankton, the Helianx were able to convert selected wavelengths of incoming cosmic rays into the energy needed to shepherd their massive bodies through the waters of their home planet. They fed by basking on the surface of the single vast ocean that encircled their world, absorbing the life-giving rays while singing their wild songs and sharing the poetry of Creation. It was a secure, benign, and loving existence in which these enormous creatures, cast alone as the sole intelligent beings of their water world, idled away the generations in philosophical speculation.

Similar to the Earth's *Cetacea,* once the Helianx had developed their environment to an optimum degree, they had little need to create complex structures external to themselves. Their inner lives were rich enough. The stability of their existence was ensured by their ability to control their population to maintain a perfectly balanced ecosystem. And by virtue of their passive, photosynthetic approach to feeding, their world was entirely free of predation. The small aquatic creatures living alongside the Helianx fed off the seaweed that grew in all its magnificent profusion covering the rocks in the shallower waters.

Knowing little of fear and free from the need to hunt for food or to work for their subsistence, the Helianx had the leisure to develop what has been generally considered to be one of the most advanced poetic cultures in the known Multiverse.

Being telepathically bonded into one large clan also allowed the Helianx the ability to receive signals from other worlds as they lay in their magickal configurations on the surface of the water. The silicate crystalline structure of their bodies, resonating as one in their meditations, acted as a single homogenous receiving station linking them to the *Universe Broadcast Circuits* and the essential awareness that they were part of a much larger Multiverse than even they could conceive.

Evolution wrought its wonders
as waves of improbable monstrosities
gave way at last to the mutation
most successfully adapted to life
on Womb Planet.

Not unlike Earth's whales,
this race lived under the great seas
which covered all but a few small islands
on this bleak and barren planet.

Gales constantly swept the surface, while
underneath, all was peaceful.

That is...

...until the seas themselves
mysteriously started to dry up.

F6-2416

I don't suffer
fools gladly...
but I do gladly
make fools suffer

5

Due to the lack of predation on Womb Planet, together with their ability to manipulate their own biology and the extreme security of their underwater world, individual Helianx life-span had steadily increased over the generations to as much as two million years in some cases. This massively extended lifetimes allowed them the luxury of learning. Over time they discovered that as they lay on the surface of the ocean they were able to receive the wisdom gained from the hard experience of millions of races living on as many worlds. Their great crystalline bodies resonated with the insights of other intelligent species. Projected images danced on wavelengths just within their field of perception, acting out the dreams and nightmares of a myriad of species on planets at a thousand different degrees of development.

Information pouring down to the Helianx was absorbed, pondered, and picked over endlessly. It was then compared with all that was previously known and originally stored in the virtually limitless memory banks of the combined neural network of the Helianx.

Since the Helianx soaked up their life energy, their food, from the twin suns around which their home planet orbited, they cannot be regarded as true aquatic creatures. This factor served them well when they finally realized their ocean was diminishing in size and depth; their world was literally drying up.

The Helianx had become the masters of survival on their utopian planet. The only extension to the richness of their inner lives that they permitted themselves were large organic computers that they modeled on their brains and cultivated from their own DNA and life plasm. Their ability to manipulate their internal biology combined with their musical sensitivities, had allowed them, after thousands of years of experimentation, to use sound as a tool. In the denser medium of water, sound waves become very real and tangible. Just as another species might use frequency modulated radio waves to convey information, so the Helianx used focused sound waves to form and shape biological matter into the complex mechanisms of their immense computers.

One of the great challenges to extremely long life spans is memory. There is simply too much to remember. It was this that had first impelled the Helianx to create their computers. Thus, these elaborate biological mechanisms stored all that the many generations of Helianx had learned about themselves, as well as the information they had accumulated over the millions of years of eavesdropping on the Universe Broadcast Circuits.

Tragically, it was these computers that were among the first things to fail while the temperature of the water gradually heated up and the seas started to evaporate.

Suddenly,

within a mere half-a-million years,
this secure and long-lived species had
no choice but to slither out onto the
rapidly growing landmass
and attempt
to fend for themselves.

A few generations of terrible losses,
their numbers dwindling from
a stable two hundred and ten
to fifty-eight, resulted in a race
of large,
white,
and understandably
grouchy,
centipedes.

Over the hundreds of millions of years of their history the Helianx had achieved a state of balance with their planet. They had succeeded in evolving the perfect physical form for their environment and the preservation of all life on their world.

When the Elders amongst the Helianx had realized that the ocean was drying up they charged all who remained of their race to gather together for one complete orbit in every ten of their intertwined twin suns. During this time they were to bond their mental energies into one metaphysical standing wave and then start the exhausting process of downloading what they could from their biological computers before the machinery had completely failed. Unfortunately, it was too little, too late. Only a fraction of the immense amount of information was successfully transferred to the bioelectronic standing wave in the Helianx own memory banks before the computers had finally spluttered and died.

Poetry and the knowledge of the ages tends to become irrelevant to a species facing immediate extinction. For the Helianx the heat was on--quite literally. What had been an easygoing life, gently moving around their almost limitless underwater world, rising to the surface only intermittently to feed and to soak up the dreams and hopes of a sentient universe before returning to the deeps to ponder and assimilate what they had learned--all this, they knew, was soon to change quite irrevocably.

Never in their previous experience, in all their explorations, had they heard of an entire biosphere disappearing almost overnight. A note: it actually took almost two hundred thousand years for the entire evaporation to complete itself. However, to the long-lived Helianx--and by that time some of their life-spans had reached three million years--those two hundred thousand years felt like they passed in a flurry of horror.

Many of the Elders were amongst the first to die. The most ancient of them, their bodies weary from millennia of service, had found themselves no longer mentally nimble enough to modify their physical forms. It was the younger ones, with the notable exception of a few remarkably quick-witted Elders, who had found that they were able to accelerate the growth of small legs by focused intention. Coded into their ancient songs were stories of when their species first discovered that they could manipulate matter with focused sound waves. This astonishing revelation was quickly followed by a rapid expansion in medical practices, in particular, this included genetic modifications that they practiced almost for the fun of it--for the novelty of inhabiting new and different physical forms. Within a few tens of millions of years they had tired of this and had stabilized their great bodies.

Thus, it was many millions of years later, when this period had been long forgotten and was stored only as trinary digits in their computers, that catastrophe had struck their planet and the seas had started to disappear.

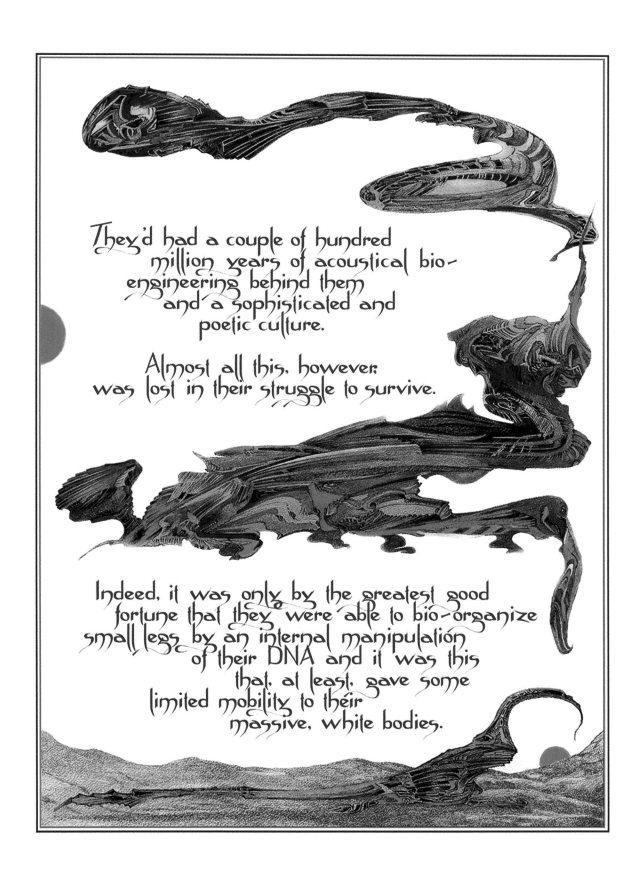

They'd had a couple of hundred
million years of acoustical bioengineering behind them
and a sophisticated and
poetic culture.

Almost all this, however,
was lost in their struggle to survive.

Indeed, it was only by the greatest good
fortune that they were able to bio-organize
small legs by an internal manipulation
of their DNA and it was this
that, at least, gave some
limited mobility to their
massive, white bodies.

Never an aggressive species, the centipedes, now known in the hiways and byways of intergalactic infinitude as THE HELIANX decided without further ado to leave Womb Planet, by now an abominably inhospitable desert.

The finer nature of physical matter in the second superuniverse allowed the Helianx a certain degree of latitude when they first found their seas disappearing. Since they drew their sustenance directly from cosmic rays, they were able to stay alive while spreading their massive bodies over the rapidly growing land masses and slithering from sea to sea. Their immense bulk made this an exhausting affair. Many of the ensuing deaths resulted from the inability of the weaker Helianx to summon the requisite energy to move their vast bodies into the receding waters before they were consumed by the heat.

It was fortunate for them that their oldest computers were located in the deepest parts of their ocean--the least affected by the rising temperatures. After some frantic, last-minute tinkering they had been able to download long-forgotten instructions on the techniques that their ancestors had perfected to produce rapid mutations. This sonic technology had allowed them to equip some of the hardier of the surviving Elders with biological extensions, small legs with which they were able to haul their enormous bodies out over the sand bars that were now separating their ocean into a multitude of smaller seas.

It was the younger and more mentally agile amongst the species who found they were able to create small legs for themselves by applying the same focus yet using conscious intention rather than sound waves to grow and nurture their limbs. The nanobots that patrolled the veins of all Helianx could well have achieved the same results, but time was pressing in for them and the 'bots' laborious technique of building organisms molecule by molecule would have taken far too long.

By this time the Helianx had theorized that the cause of the disaster was the explosion of a nearby star. This had sent waves of heat expanding out through space, which stripped the uninhabited planets of water and any signs of early life, before finally dissipating. The Helianx were well aware that such cosmic events had been known to occur, they had heard the gossip going around the universe broadcast circuits. But, as far as they could establish, such devastating cosmic convulsions were relatively rare and when they did happen they took place in *unpervaded space*. In spite of the chatter on the broadcast circuits, no sentient beings, or indeed, inhabited planets, were known to have been overly influenced by such a potential disaster. It had not been much comfort for the Helianx to realize they might have been the first race to be driven from their planet of origin.

Luckily Womb Planet was not amongst those worlds closest to the nova, and it was even more fortunate for the Helianx that one of the twin stars around which their planet orbited, had blocked the worst impact of the explosion. Although much of the surface of the sea had evaporated in the original blast, due to the extreme depth of the ocean, many of the Helianx were able to survive long enough to form a plan.

Never an aggressive species,
the centipedes,
now known in the hiways and byways
of intergalactic infinitude as

THE
HELIANX

decided without further
ado to leave Womb Planet,
by now an abominably
inhospitable desert.

The space glider, an immense biomorphic structure, was first created as an astral hologram in the collective, creative imagination of the Helianx.

Over the aeons, this race had excelled at co-creating tremendous theatrical productions, entirely in their collective imagination. Each individual Helianx was able to visualize the elaborate performance projected on their *eidetic screens*, adding their own idiosyncratic touches as the show developed. Not only were these performances endlessly entertaining, but they were the main way by which the Helianx kept the long history of their race as a living tradition, with each individual participating in shaping the overall vision.

So important were these psychic extravaganzas to the Helianx that considerable effort was put into training their young in the art of manipulating and transforming *astral energies* into the grosser frequency of consensus reality. They were helped in this by being able to work with *liquid light*, a technique they had adopted after hearing about it on the broadcast circuits from another advanced species.

In this manner all Helianx eventually became skilled at playfully molding, and then downstepping, small packets of astral energy, using sonic holography to further crystallize the higher frequencies into material reality. However, creating, and then manifesting, something as large as the space glider had never been attempted before.

As the design grew in size and complexity, each individual Helianx held the image as an astral hologram, floating freely in the group mind. When they had completed the modifications and incorporated all the ideas of the best thinkers of their race, they placed the Great Ship in orbit around their planet on the lower astral frequencies. Then, with the gentle help and encouragement of an invisible agency that the Helianx had long acknowledged as the *Supreme Being*, and by dint of what they could only imagine as *celestial collaboration*, the Helianx found themselves able collectively to lower the vibrational frequency of their enormous imagined craft so as to allow it to exist within their physical reality.

Having spent so much of their long lives as an underwater species, the Helianx were particularly aware of the multilayered structure of the Multiverse. Also, throughout their extensive history of out-of-the-body travel they had come to appreciate the vast abundance of life on virtually every frequency available. It was this knowledge that had encouraged the Helianx to take on the frantic final effort to extract themselves from a seemingly impossible situation.

Time was getting short and the twin suns of Womb Planet burnt down relentlessly on a world that was rapidly dying--through no fault of its unfortunate inhabitants. Not surprisingly, this created a deep and lasting psychic scar on this ancient race, mitigated somewhat by the wisdom of the Elders, who pointed out that they might well have needed this sharp jolt to get them off Womb Planet and out and into the vast physical Multiverse, to meet an entirely new destiny.

Within fifty thousand years they had created a vast, translucent space glider, one million miles in length. It hung in geosynchronous orbit around their planet...

...at the very limit
of their acoustic capabilities.

Until, in one last
racial spasm,
they hurled
themselves
up...

to join the spider,
abandoning their
world behind
them in the
process.

The computers predicted a high probability that the immense psychic energies required for the Helianx to project themselves up and out to join their ship would result in the destruction of their planet. A search of their voluminous memory banks revealed that almost nothing was known about high energy transduction on this scale, but it was logical to anticipate that such a violent act would, of necessity, have equally violent repercussions.

After sober consideration of the deteriorating state of their world, by this time a nearly waterless desert, they all felt that the risk was worthwhile. If the worst was to happen, then they would have to concern themselves with that later. Despite the steadily worsening conditions, this was not an easy decision to take since the Helianx dearly loved their world. It had birthed and nurtured them, and they had gratefully thought of it as their collective womb.

Unlike the space-faring species who roamed the pervaded spaces of the superuniverse, the Helianx had been more than happy to stay on their world throughout their long history of sentience. Their ability to travel the inner worlds seemed to satisfy their desire for novelty and they had traditionally considered any idea of heaving their large bodies into space as idiotic--and, besides, it would be well beneath their dignity. But beneath this conservative world-view there had always lurked a deep unease. Granted, their highly developed mental abilities allowed them to travel the Multiverse in out-of-the-body states, but this had also fed a growing frustration. While they were able to move freely through the astral regions of the inhabited worlds of the second superuniverse, they were unable to interact in any way with what they observed. The Helianx were not able, or willing, to attempt to match their vibrational frequency with that of the world they were visiting, and very wisely, too. The sudden appearance in their midst of a two-mile-long mountain of embarrassed flesh would be bound to disturb the serenity of even the most sophisticated species. The Helianx chose sensibly to remain firmly in the astral.

As a result of this cloak of invisibility, the Helianx came to be thought of as cosmic eavesdroppers, and by some even as agents of espionage, as they flitted delicately through the astral realms of the worlds that interested them. The fascination that drove them on to explore inhabited planets was their race's obsession with bardic poetry: they reveled in discovering how the myriad sentient species accounted for themselves; their belief systems and creation myths; their arts and philosophies, and most of all, their senses of humor.

The Helianx had tried to make sure their information was of limited value to the few belligerent species who had developed their telepathic abilities sufficiently enough to detect the Space Gypsies' invisible presence, and had attempted to communicate with them. Unfortunately, their undeservedly dubious reputation had become almost impossible to shake off. It has been said that on some worlds the very mention of the name Helianx was enough to scare children into silence. Yet in their own collective mind these gentle giants had always considered their intentions as benign and utterly harmless.

...at the very limit of their acoustic capabilities.

Until, in one last racial spasm, they hurled themselves up...

...to join the glider, atomizing their world behind them in the process.

The space glider proved to be the salvation of the Helianx for more reasons than obvious. Nil-gravity space was greeted with delirious happiness not only for the aerobatic possibilities, but more simply because it took the weight off their feet - their poor pathetically crumpled, swollen, sore, sore, sore, feet.

The numero uno problem on their home planet's so recently existent surface.

Any species of sentient life will have a wide disparity of reactions to a sudden change of biosphere, however carefully their new home is modeled on their previously stable environment. It had been no different for the Helianx, despite the obsessive attention they had given to the design of what was to become their floating world for the unforeseeable future.

It was natural for the Helianx to hope that Womb Planet would withstand the intense energies that built up when they projecting themselves up to join the glider, but as they clustered to the viewing portals they could see their planet disintegrating beneath them. Deeply disturbed by the sight, their group mind oscillating wildly between horror and relief, the Helianx slowly came to realize what they had most feared: that there was no turning back. Their placid, easygoing lives were never going to be the same again. It was then that the wisdom of their Elders in counseling the many thoughtful details and enormous size of the ship had dawned on those who theorized that they should be able to return in time to Womb Planet, if indeed it did survive their exodus, and then aqua-form the barren world to suit their needs.

However, much of their trepidation faded in the joy of the success of meeting their impossible challenge, as well as the immediate relief of nil-gravity space. Memories of their race's recent exile from the supportive luxury of water to the living hell of having to scrabble over dry land, dissipated quickly in the pleasures of a gravity-free life.

Throughout its long period of evolution the lack of any sort of predation on Womb Planet had created in the Helianx a species that had never been subject to the extremes of fear. Their planet was also way off the normal superuniverse trade routes which had ensured that they were seldom visited. No aggressive species had ever discovered the whereabouts of Womb Planet. The enormous size of the Helianx and the apparent inhospitality of a water-world constantly swept by intense storms was enough to discourage the few races who might have stumbled inadvertently on the planet.

It should be remembered that in those early days of Multiverse development, when the planets in the first and second superuniverses had been seeded with life, there was far less travel between the worlds amongst the more advanced intelligent species. Most inhabited planets were linked by embedded broadcast circuitry that transmitted realtime holograms at the speed of thought, and which allowed the beings in those sectors of space to stay in contact with one another. The enormous cost of energy and resources demanded by space travel in the physical superuniverse made the enterprise much less attractive when the exploration of other worlds was pointless. The use of localized wormhole technology and hyper-space drives to transit the vast intergalactic distances did not come until a much later era in Multiverse evolution.

The space glider proved to be the salvation of
the Helianx for more reasons than obvious.
Nil-gravity space was greeted with delirious
happiness, not only for the aerobatic possibilities,
but more simply because it took the weight off
their feet - their poor, pathetically crumpled,
swollen, sore,
sore, sore,
feet.

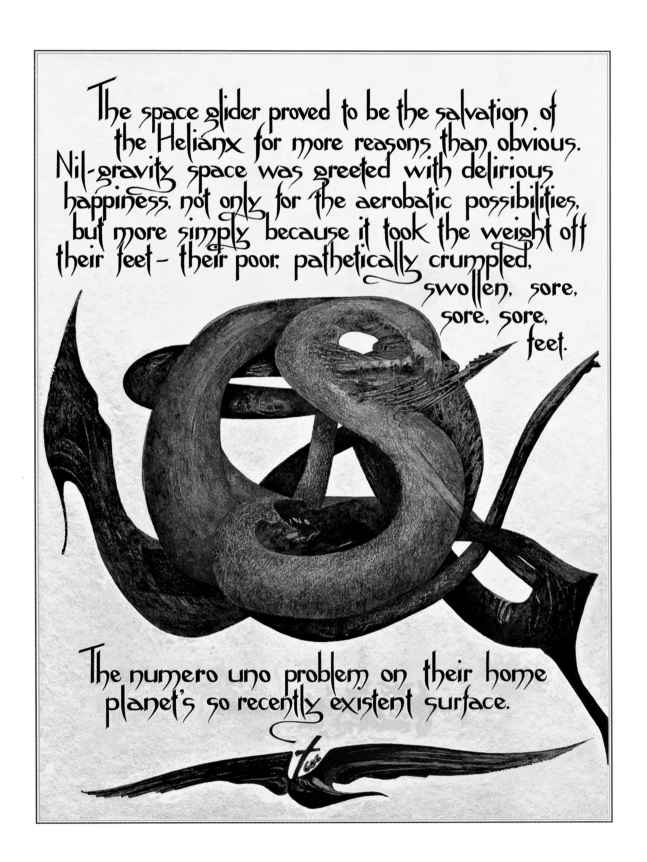

The numero uno problem on their home
planet's so recently existent surface.

The catastrophe that had precipitated the Helianx off their planet and into space, and that had so thoroughly destroyed their world, made them a rarity amongst the multitude of intelligent species of the second superuniverse. There were a few races who found it necessary, generally for social or political reasons, to invest their collective assets in space travel, but due to their limited life-spans they seldom ventured far from their own solar systems. Consequently, there were no real space-faring traditions within the confines of the two original superuniverses until much later, when wormhole transit technology emerged as a result of psychic practices of the Helianx.

The Helianx inadvertently became one of the few exceptions, their exceptionally long lifetimes allowing them the luxury of drifting on the cosmic winds from star to star. When they had located a world to study, they secured the Great Ship in orbit around the planet and attempted to open up diplomatic relations telepathically. In most cases they knew what they would find since these were planetary cultures upon which the Helianx had spied in their out-of-the-body adventures. Once diplomatic overtures were completed the envoys of the host culture were given the choice to be teleported up to the luxurious meeting chambers of the Great Ship for face-to-face exchanges.

Certain risks were involved with teleportation and this was explained along with a self-effacing warning as to what to expect on first sight of the Helianx. Due to their inconvenient size and their dislike of the effects of gravity, the Helianx had made a rule to never descend to the surface of a host planet, and this only added to the sense of mystery surrounding these galactic wanderers. The extraordinary size of the space glider, the alien luxury of the surroundings, and the high weirdness of the Helianx themselves, were well-nigh impossible to describe when the envoys returned to their own cultures.

It was in this way that the legend of the Helianx grew amongst the many peoples they visited. Having spent so much of their previous existence traveling out-of-the-body and peeking ineffectually into the lives of other beings, there was a particular delight for the Helianx in the pure physicality of these exchanges. They found that there was so much more that could be accomplished by direct communication with other races than could ever be discovered by hovering around in the astral, half-hoping they would overhear something they considered significant.

Yet, despite the frightening disparity between the size of the Helianx and that of the planetary representatives, the visiting envoys invariably found a charming and interested audience amongst the immense creatures. Well-fed and lavishly entertained, the planetary ambassadors were more than willing to discuss the social and philosophical issues that were engaging the best minds of their world.

In this way the Helianx became the first of the early cosmic cultural anthropologists, accumulating vast libraries of holographic recordings of the many thousands of cooperative intelligent species they encountered.

Having had
recent reasons to
become a more audacious species,
and by now not overly tied to secure &
stable environments, they took happily and
naturally to their new peripatetic
function of universal
wanderers.

They moved from galaxy to galaxy
and solar system to solar system, singing
their cool, dry songs of space.

Magical entities, the Helianx became
the custodians of the belief systems of all
the sentient species they encountered,
eagerly cataloguing and cross-referencing
the abstract speculations of the philosophers of
a thousand thousand races.

What had begun for the Helianx as the pure delight of flitting in their space glider from inhabited planet to inhabited planet, making contact with all the intelligent species they came across and gathering their belief systems, became, over time, a far more serious affair.

Patterns started to emerge as the Helianx assimilated and pared down more and more of the accumulated wisdom of the beings they encountered. These patterns, although admittedly adding a depth of poignancy to the songs their computers wove for them, also resulted in planting a seed of concern in their group-mind. Easygoing and mild by nature and happily relaxed by the long, indolent, journeys between the star systems, the Helianx were able to repress this vague sense of unease in much the same way as they had attempted to put the demise of their planet out of their collective mind.

Some contemporary galactic *exopsychologists*, in their recent studies of the Helianx, have pointed out the inadvisability of ignoring such profound trauma by repressing the memory of such pain. They have suggested that the growing intensity of Helianx research may well have been fueled by the slow and inevitable abreaction to the terrifying event in their past. These exopsychologists have further theorized that hearing firsthand of the many trials and tribulations faced by other emerging planetary cultures may have encouraged the Helianx, over time, to come to terms with their own near extinction. The more sympathetic amongst these social scientists have also proposed that the lack of predation on Womb Planet--the very factor which had allowed the Helianx such placid, pleasant lives--had ill-prepared them for the extremes of negative emotion they were bound to experience in the course of such a catastrophe. They point out that the challenges faced by a species that has to fight its way up the intelligence tree will tend to favor individuals of that species with greatly strengthened *emotional bodies*.

The Helianx, physically enormous and powerfully intelligent and capable of group-mind melding while retaining individual consciousness, soon became known for their emotionally immature and mischievous natures. To some of the races that the Space Gypsies visited, this ambiguity, this seemingly paradoxical quality of consciousness, caused some confusion when they came to study the new songs the Helianx had brought with them. Yet it was often out of this intellectual tumult that emergent cultures would reach new pinnacles of understanding and for that they were generally grateful to their strange visitors.

For the Helianx themselves, the effect they created on inhabited worlds was of little importance in the light of their own central question--the issue that had started to preoccupy them while they slowly came to terms with their fate as exiles from paradise.

They would analyze the rhythms
and underlying meanings
on their voluminous bio-computers,
reconstituting the results
into long, finely-woven, songs.

Each belief system added its own
particular idiosyncrasy as the songs of
the Helianx grew
in depth and complexity.

Other races
waited with bated breathing
systems for their next visit,
wondering what new additions
to the 'space gypsies' repertoire
might help them resolve
the most profound problem
facing all of life,
everywhere...

Galactic social engineers have long noted that intelligent species, evolving under particularly benign conditions, tend over time to slip into intellectual and spiritual complacency. Life is too easy; the challenges, too few.

The Helianx had been more than content to bask in the golden light of their two suns and to dive and play in the cool depth of Mother Ocean. Living long, languorous lives, their joy and fascination derived mainly from the complex subtleties embedded within even the most trivial of encounters between members of a telepathic race. The Helianx had never given much time to the deeper questions that beset all creatures capable of pondering their own existence.

Since they were a mature species they had long since learned how to control their population and had chosen to follow a tradition of keeping their number to a stable 210, a level they felt their biosphere could comfortably support on Womb Planet. As an inevitable consequence, this limiting factor, as well as their exceptionally long lives, required individual Helianx to become masters of diplomacy. Constant attention to the state of the telepathic *Web* that linked all Helianx into one coherent group mind demanded a rare sensitivity to the needs of others. The slightest shift in consciousness of a single Helianx directly impacted on all, needing constant adjustments in each of their *psychospheres* while they juggled their psychic energies to bring the Web back into equilibrium.

It had not always been this way. The Helianx had developed telepathy as a natural result of being an aquatic species, water being a much more efficient carrier medium than air for subtle energies. Although the evolution of an effective group mind occurred many generations before the catastrophe, the legends coded into the songs of the Helianx still spoke of a time when individuals floated alone and isolated one from another. Locked within their own psychospheres and trapped in mountains of blubber, they were able to communicate with each other only through their songs and the movement of their massive bodies. It was a long, lonely and frustrating epoch in the history of their species.

Telepathy had come to them gradually when the younger and more experimental amongst them had started exploring the possibility of overlaying their elaborate songs with sonic holograms. Over time, they discovered the sound waves that they were capable of generating were able to carry far more information than the mere meaning of the song. With discipline and after much practice, they discovered they could create coherent visual thoughtforms within their own psychospheres, which could be transmitted over the sound waves. As musicians might communicate a wide range of subtle feelings by the way they modulate the sound created, so the Helianx found themselves gradually able to deepen their contact with one another to a previously unfathomable degree.

It was the start of a new era in social relationships for the Helianx and had led directly to the creation of the Web and to their ability to travel collectively out of their massive bodies.

The catastrophe that had befallen Womb Planet and the terrible losses amongst the Helianx that had resulted from the burning off of their ocean, not surprisingly, had created a violent destabilization in the integrity of the Web. The sensitive network simply had not been able to cope with the strength of the emotions produced by so much death and had collapsed, leaving the horrified Helianx driven back into the isolation of their own individual psychospheres. It had only been by summoning up the last of their collective psychic resources that they had been able to teleport themselves up into the space glider.

Once the Helianx had secured themselves on the ship it had taken many generations for them to harmonize the Web and to start to build up their numbers again, before they felt confident enough to launch off on their endless journey through the Multiverse. Aimlessly they had circled the space where their planet had so recently existed, licking their wounds, both physical and psychic, while they tried to grow accustomed to their new home. Certainly they had the advantage of knowing the layout beforehand, since all of them collaboratively had designed and created the Great Ship. But holding a design in the realm of the collective imagination remains very different from actually swimming through the cavernous chambers and capacious corridors that threaded, like massive intestines, throughout the length of the ship. The cool depths, designed to emulate Mother Ocean and held in place by the slow rotation of the craft, yielded naturally to huge transparent bubbles. These nutrient chambers were molded with the surface of the Great Ship to allow the Helianx to soak in the nutritive cosmic rays.

As might be imagined, the urgency demanded by the oncoming catastrophe stimulated the inventive and creative faculties of the Helianx, and concentrated their minds to a wonderful extent. Issues they had placidly taken for granted for aeons were reexamined in the light of their impending planetary exodus. They knew their collective survival depended on getting every detail of the craft correct first time. Fortunately they had the ability to test the reliability of their designs by simulating the conditions of deep space in their powerful group mind and modifying the craft as necessary.

This led to some startling discoveries, amongst which the most reassuring was their realization that it was not from their twin suns that they gained their sustenance, but from cosmic rays that appeared to emanate from the center of the Multiverse. Thus, these rays would be bound to be present throughout the spacetime continuum. This revelation answered their most worrying question, because had it not been so the Helianx would have been condemned to be prisoners of their own solar system, endlessly orbiting their two parent suns.

Their main concern, however, had been finally settled. The constant presence of these benign cosmic rays would ensure their survival wherever they traveled, and most importantly, they would be able to continue their pursuit of truth amongst the intelligent species they hoped they would meet in their adventures.

24

As all questions can be answered
in the fullness of time,
it was no surprise to the Helianx when,
after the addition of the two hundred and ten million,
one hundred and forty fourth belief system,
their almost centipedean computers started
coughing out, not the usual, plaintive notes
of yet another melody,
but a most disturbing message.

No sort of complete answer to the original
question, mind you, but a part of the puzzle
that the Helianx had
secretly dreaded.

In those early days of the Multiverse, most species intelligent enough to consider their own natures had a natural awareness of a universal Creator. Its mysterious Presence seemed to surround them. There was no need for priests or religious instruction on most worlds since mature beings almost always developed a direct inner link with the Being they thought of as the *First Source and Center* of all that existed. Life for these species became a series of initiations, each challenge they met appeared to yield a deeper intuition of this mysterious Presence that seemed to be so powerful and, at the same time, so subtle and gentle. A tenderness these enormous entities could barely contain.

And yet, because all sentient life possesses innate curiosity, unanswered questions were bound to arise as they examined the philosophical and moral issues that are so important to intelligent beings. This questioning invariably led to the central quandary facing all thoughtful beings: Given the experiential reality of a loving and benign Creator, why do such painful, destructive events occur?

For the Helianx, of course, this conundrum had a particular depth of meaning, because it touched the very core of their collective trauma. The solipsistic meditations on the meaning of life which had so preoccupied them in their long evolutionary history on Womb Planet were rendered virtually pointless in the face of a disaster that they considered horrifyingly arbitrary. When everything seemed to revolve around them and nothing intervened to threaten their existence, they could never have even conceived of such a global calamity. Not only was their belief in a stable and friendly Multiverse severely tested, but the shock of having to drag their enormous, clumsy bodies over the emerging land masses had introduced them to pain and suffering on a level they would never have previously thought possible. The small legs they had managed to develop were barely able to scrabble under the huge weight of the creatures as gravity bore down on them. Wholly unused to this new pressure, their legs crushed and bloody beneath them, many had simply given up the bitter struggle and had allowed themselves to disintegrate back into their myriad constituent tiny organisms.

By the time the surviving Helianx managed to gather the last of their life energies and had teleported themselves up to the Great Ship, they had become a rather different species. Although their reputation would always be colored by those easygoing early years on Womb Planet, something inside them had hardened. Fear and doubt of a sort that they had never experienced before had now entered their lives.

When they had recovered somewhat from their ordeal and had set out on their journey in the Great Ship, the Helianx found that a new urgency now fueled their questioning of all the races they met. Afterwards, they would gather and anxiously await the new songs that their stupendous computers spat out after yet another belief system had been assimilated, examined, compared, and extrapolated for any clues as to what their collective destiny might be.

When some answers finally did emerge the Helianx were already skeptical enough not to be surprised to learn of even more perilous times to come.

In short,
their planetside problem
of sore extremities
represented a very real
physical vulnerability
soon to catch up with them
unless they managed some
fancy footwork.

Just as most thoughtful species attempt to examine their origins, the more advanced amongst them in those early days also enthusiastically explored what their futures might hold. Some contemporary cosmologists have theorized that the *spacetime continuum* was more fluid, more malleable perhaps, more intimately entwined with the consciousness of the beings who inhabited the superuniverses in those times. These conditions appeared to have made it possible for the few adepts amongst the different races, who had achieved this state of union with the All, to gain brief glimpses into the future.

However, it was also the very plasticity of the temporal and physical substance of the cosmos that tended to make their prognostications unreliable. Not only did freedom of choice invariably enter the picture to make any prediction inherently fallible, but in many situations the collective consciousness of the concerned species made the necessary corrections to avoid the anticipated disaster, without any help from seers or prophets. Any vision of the future, the philosophers of most races came to believe, was based on the probability of an event occurring as an extrapolation of innumerable current factors and conditions--and those can always change with surprising speed.

There were always a few recorded situations in which these predictive visions had acted as a valuable warning and had allowed the race concerned to take the appropriate actions to avoid a coming catastrophe. Whether or not these cases were purely the result of good fortune, evidently they had occurred with sufficient frequency to pique the interest of the Helianx. In spite of their proficiency in the psychic arts, they had received absolutely no warnings of the global calamity that had now changed their lives forever.

In the light of this unfortunate lacuna in what the Helianx had come to consider with some pride as their particular area of expertise, it had seemed supremely ironic to them that it was only after the addition of the cosmology of just one of these races that their computers had finally reached a conclusion in their galaxy-wide analysis of probable futures. In actuality, the determination at which the computers had arrived did not directly address the central issue that had so obsessed the Helianx: that of the deeper cause behind the catastrophe that had destroyed their precious world?

What they did learn turned out to be far more startling than any answer they might have received to this question and directly concerned the many intelligent species in the superuniverse. The rhythmic expansion and contraction of the spacetime continuum, or so the computers appeared to be counseling, would subject all matter to increasingly powerful gravitational forces as the Multiverse unfolded.

Not information of great interest to most short-lived species, but to a race that had become virtually immortal and whose bodies, though large, were structurally appallingly delicate, it was a terrifying prospect.

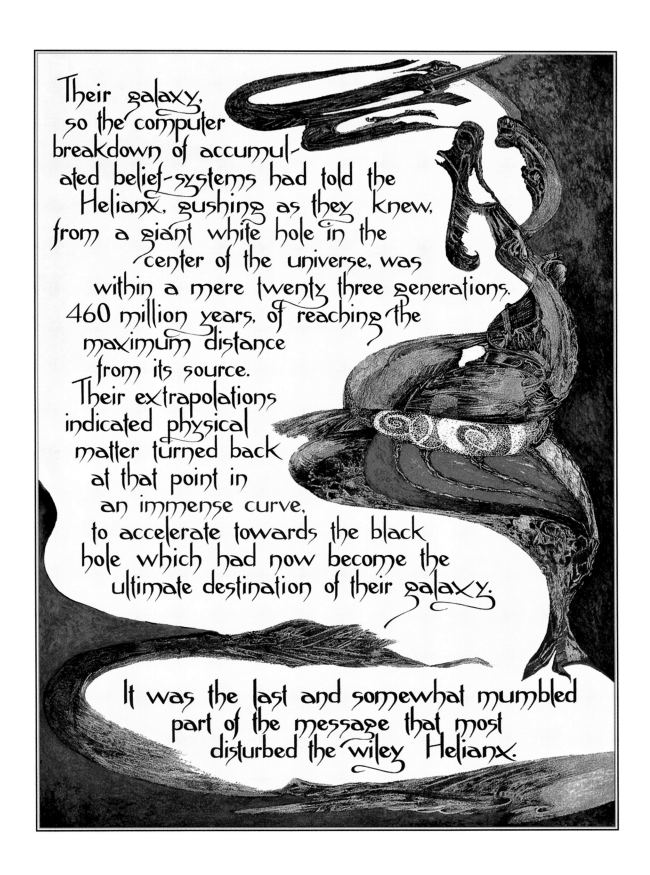

Their galaxy,
so the computer
breakdown of accumul-
ated belief-systems had told the
Helianx, gushing as they knew,
from a giant white hole in the
center of the universe, was
within a mere twenty three generations,
460 million years, of reaching the
maximum distance
from its source.
Their extrapolations
indicated physical
matter turned back
at that point in
an immense curve,
to accelerate towards the black
hole which had now become the
ultimate destination of their galaxy.

It was the last and somewhat mumbled
part of the message that most
disturbed the wiley Helianx.

Life for the Helianx in the course of their long journey on the Great Ship through the vastness of the superuniverse had become increasingly easygoing, as the persistent reverberations of the explosive exodus from their planetary home gradually diminished in their collective memory. Unfortunately, old habits started to reassert themselves as the enormous creatures lazed away the galactic night in the dreaming chambers on the ship. Once the initial excitement of meeting other species face to face, as it were, had subsided, the Helianx tended to slip back into their previous ways. This mood was compounded by the immense distances that generally separated different star systems, each with their inhabited worlds. However fascinating their encounters in the flesh had been, they also had considerable limitations.

The Helianx soon found that their sheer physical size, which was not an issue when they were traveling in an out-of-the-body state, was so vastly different from almost all the species they met in their travels that it tended to make communication somewhat unrewarding. The very size of the Great Ship was enough to inhibit all but the most urbane of planetary envoys and there was little the Helianx could do to disguise their own appearance. The ship's translation devices, by reducing the volume and bandwidth used by the Helianx in non-telepathic mode, made sure that their complex soundings could be heard and understood by those envoys who had overcome their initial terror.

This disappointing tendency led to even greater efforts by the Helianx to soften the negative effects they had on those with whom they had managed to establish contact. After a few unfortunate encounters they repressed even more firmly the intensity of their desire to understand what had happened to their world, and how, in a benign Creation, such a thing might have been permitted to occur.

They immersed themselves in the subtleties of those cosmologies that particularly intrigued them, giving themselves so selflessly to the task that their very sense of themselves-- always somewhat tenuous, as with most telepathic species--gradually started to dissipate. Without quite realizing how it had taken place they found themselves less and less inclined to continue their explorations. The songs that issued from the computers had become increasingly mournful over time as the shape-of-things-to-come slowly formed within their prodigal circuitry.

As has been the case with many technologically savvy species, over time the Helianx had allowed themselves to become increasingly reliant on their sophisticated tools. So different from their simple lives on Womb Planet, this unfortunate dependence had led, in turn, to a further weakening in the life-force of the creatures.

All of which made it even more shocking when their computers finally predicted that their gelatinous bodies would not be able to survive the gravitational stresses of such a massive reversal in the spacetime continuum.

The computers coughed
and spluttered…

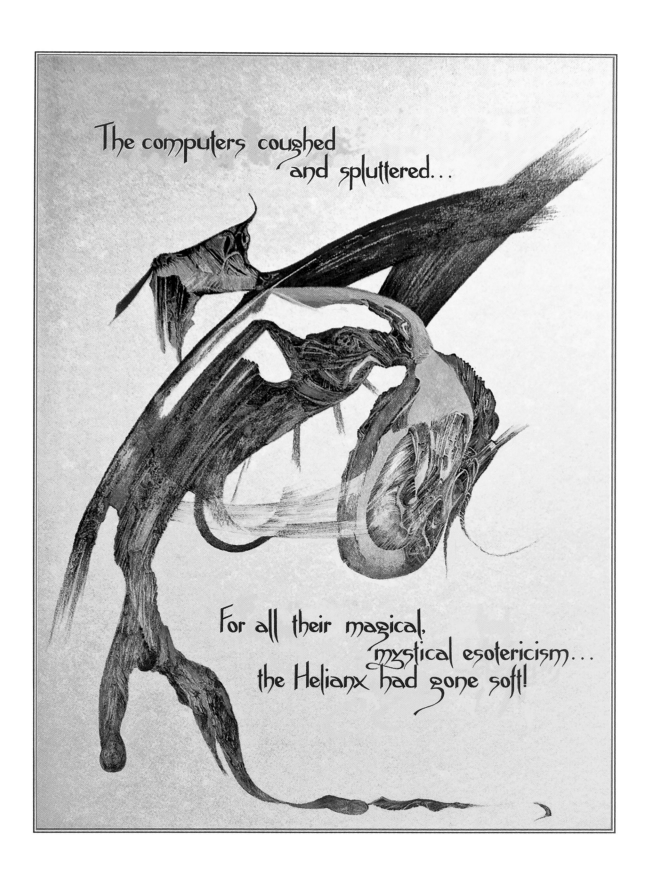

For all their magical,
mystical esotericism…
the Helianx had gone soft!

Always an altruistic species, the Helianx drew one last sweep through the inhabited universe sensing their some of the long return home. A warning, if you like, a statement an observation they sincerely hoped would be heard and understood by all. Their message, however, was received with a wide disparity of reactions. Some thought it unnecessary, alarmist. 460 million years!

The Helianx had sorely needed to pull themselves together and take some definitive action if they were to continue to exist. The shocking news their computers had been so embarrassed to tell them continued to reverberate through their collective consciousness, reactivating the trauma they had tried so hard to repress. Evolutionarily unaccustomed to such powerful negative emotions, and yet now faced by a second-- manifestly earthshaking--cosmic drama, the Helianx found themselves forced to come to terms with what seemed to be their destiny and did their best to put their concerns aside.

Their extensive researches into the natural history of all those millions of species they had visited in their travels around the superuniverse had convinced them that, with very few exceptions, they had been the only race of intelligent beings who had managed to leave their planet before their biosphere was destroyed. The few exceptions, however, were those worlds in which the mass extinction of life had occurred before the planetary inhabitants had become aware of what was happening, and these catastrophes the Helianx had only heard about from their occasional encounters with other space-faring explorers.

Realizing that a few other worlds had suffered the same fate had helped mitigate the sense the Helianx had that they had been unfairly selected by forces they had not understood, for a singular and horrible end. And as they pondered the recent information on the fate of the spacetime continuum, they understood that this future challenge would intimately concern all sentient life. At least, the Helianx felt, they had not been singled out this time. These hard-won realizations allowed them enough psychological breathing space once again to stabilize the Web and to help the younger Helianx, those who had not been among the original 57 to leave Womb Planet, to come to terms with a past from which they had been so thoroughly cloaked by their Elders. Fearful of passing on the brunt of the trauma they had undergone, the surviving Elders had delayed the decision to procreate until they had so firmly repressed the painful memories that barely a trace remained in the Web.

It was many millions of years before the Helianx had managed to restore sufficient confidence in themselves and the Multiverse to think of bringing their numbers back up again to their optimal 210. Even then, they tried their best to make sure that the youngsters knew as little as possible about the true nature of the tragedy that had befallen them. The Elders felt this justified them in raising their progeny to be conscious only of their shipboard life. And when the young ones inevitably stumbled on the faint echoes of a tragic prehistory never mentioned by their teachers, the minute reverberations that continued to vibrate in the telepathic matrix had to be explained away as a vague, but mythologized, past.

All this changed, however, when the computers finally revealed their disturbing shared destiny. The Helianx now knew they had to gather all their resources to confront, and somehow to deal with, what appeared to them to be an inevitable doom.

Always an altruistic species,
the Helianx drew one last sweep
through the inhabited universe singing their
song of the long return home.
A warning, if you like, a statement,
an observation, they sincerely hoped
would be heard and understood by all.
Their message, however, was received
with a wide disparity of reactions.
Some thought it unnecessarily
alarmist...460 million years!

This mainly from the short-lived species.

Others, more daring perhaps, set out to see if they could accelerate the process while still others a trifle more pragmatic by nature, greeted the melodic masterpiece as yet another of the poetic excesses that had dogged the reputation of a race known in the past for its tendency towards placid self-indulgence.

Multiverse historians have frequently commented on the unlikely emergence of altruism in intelligent life. Although the maternal impulse in most species can lead to acts of remarkable self-sacrifice, these were seen as being strictly personal and tended to have little impact on the way societies made their decisions. While theories of kin selection can be widened to include a species behavior under a threat to its collective survival, many evolutionary biologists would argue that this is better explained as a selfish action on behalf of the species as a whole. And perhaps the decision by the Helianx to set off on yet another cosmic journey, this time to inform all the races they encountered of the ultimate fate of the spacetime continuum, was also colored by self-interest. After all, they sorely needed the time to work out what they were going to do about this new impending disaster.

Whereas reciprocal altruism between different species is occasionally seen in the simpler orders of life, by the time a planetary culture becomes aware that other intelligent races exist, it is very much in their self-interest to treat well the extraterrestrials they encounter. Knowing the levels of cooperation needed for a race to be able to develop the technology to travel between the stars, and with all they had gathered through their links with other worlds over the broadcast circuits, the planetary culture in question would have been reassured that any off-world visitation was benign.

The suffering the surviving Helianx had undergone when they had to witness their beloved companions dying in the harsh sunlight had shattered their placid, easygoing, existence. Although they were well aware of life on other planets through their out-of-the-body travels, it had taken the disaster to make real to them just how vulnerable all sentient species were to arbitrary cosmic forces. Out of this realization came the desire to warn the intelligent races they visited in the Great Ship of what they had learned of the times to come.

For the Helianx it was disappointing, but barely surprising, that their warning was so largely ignored. It was not a subject that most races wanted to think about, and besides, even if the computers' predicted timeline was accurate, no one really knew what a reversal of the spacetime continuum actually entailed for the life forms alive at that time. The computers had shown the Helianx that they would not be able to survive the extreme gravitational forces, the violent stresses would tear their massive bodies apart. Other races were quick to point out that this was unlikely to happen to them since who knew what they were destined to become, or where they were likely to be, in 460 million years. And, since even the long-lived species rarely lived for more than four or five hundred years, they were able to dismiss the forecast as of no immediate concern to them.

Refusing to be discouraged by the disinterest of other races, the Helianx could only observe this willful blindness with a sad detachment, while they continued to hatch their plans to escape their inexorable fate.

This,
    mainly from
        the short-lived species.

Others,
        more daring perhaps,
    set out to see if they could accel-
        erate the process; while still
            others, a trifle more pragmatic
        by nature, greeted the melodic
            masterpiece as yet another of the
    poetic excesses that had dogged the
reputation of a race known in the past
            for its tendency towards
            flaccid self-indulgence.

The intimate, almost symbiotic, relationship between the Helianx and their computers had proved to be a boon through their difficult last years on Womb Planet. Granted, their reliance on these intelligent biomechanisms to act as repositories for all the knowledge the Helianx had gathered had shaded, in time, into dependence, but all in all, they felt the exchange had been worthwhile. Being able to call on the vast libraries for an analysis of their situation when their ocean had started to dry up had led them directly to the design and creation of the Great Ship.

Apart from their computers, which they considered should be described more correctly as biological than mechanical, the Helianx had not been considered to be a particularly technologically advanced species prior to the calamity that destroyed their biosphere. The conditions of their underwater world naturally discouraged the need for external devices. Their out-of-the-body adventures had precluded a desire to build spaceships and their telepathic abilities had satisfied any inclination for long-distance telephony. With nutrition so easily acquired on Womb Planet, and all they ever needed readily available in the friendly seas, competition between individual Helianx was all but unknown. There was no impulse to construct dwellings, or to hoard personal belongings, since life in all its simplicity seemed to them to be fascinating enough. Conflicts and disagreements between individual Helianx, as in any sentient species, were inevitable but rare, and could always be settled on the Web before any serious physical confrontation might develop.

While this gentle tolerance of others had led naturally to many millions of years of peaceful coexistence amongst the Helianx, it had ill-prepared them for the stellar explosion that was to strip their planet of life. Another species with more highly developed technological skills and facing the same conditions, might well have tried to avoid the disaster by taking some form of preemptive action. The Helianx, struggling to come to terms with the psychic turbulence in the Web, were not equipped emotionally, or technologically, to do anything but flee the catastrophe by any means they were able to devise before it was too late.

It was in the chaos of those traumatic times that the cool detachment of their computers had proved to be so invaluable. When the Helianx had originally designed and fashioned them, they had assumed their main use would be data storage, thus relieving their creators of having to retain all they had absorbed in their astral travels. Being technically inexperienced the Helianx had not realized that their bioplasmic creations eventually would evolve a mind of their of their own-- a cool, dry, and rather judgmental mind. Its countless interconnections were created and structured from the constant complex analyses of the philosophies and belief systems of all those many millions of species that the Helianx had studied silently from their astral perches.

As they were completing this long, last tour the computers, now redundant from their usual fare, were painstakingly reprogrammed to calculate all the options open to the centipedes.

And it was out of these suggestions that the Helianx decided to pick, somewhat reluctantly, the statistically most viable course of action.

Since their computers had been so vital in developing a plan to leave Womb Planet, the Helianx once again found themselves having to rely on their bioplasmic associates to discover a way out of their new dilemma. Their altruistic impulse to spread the news of the impending reversal of the spacetime continuum to all the species they met in their journeys also had the advantage of giving the computers enough time to consider the problem in depth.

They all knew that it was not going to be easy. To even consider the idea that the very ground of their being might reverse its expanding momentum and collapse in on itself, was terrifying enough to think about in practical terms. This was certainly the view of many of the species the Helianx had tried to warn, and who consequently found it all too easy to dismiss the prediction as a whimsical fantasy; and far too far in the future for much concern, even if it might be true.

The Helianx, however, took the information a great deal more seriously. After all, their computers had already solved one seemingly imponderable situation and the Helianx could only hope that they were up to puzzling out this one, too.

What at first appeared to preoccupy the computers as they examined the unimaginable event that lay ahead, was what they had been discovering about the nature and structure of matter itself. Whereas the scientists of many of the races of that time held that matter was inherently lifeless, the Helianx computers were starting to look at the growing possibility that somewhere at the heart of matter, buried perhaps within the very smallest of the particles, lay an intelligence of an entirely different order. For the Helianx this had been hard to confront, since if matter did indeed possess an innate intelligence, then presumably there had to have been some form of intentionality behind the stellar nova that had destroyed their planet. As a consequence, they did their best to resist this notion for a long time.

It had been just as difficult for them to view the calamitous event as entirely arbitrary, as a cosmic accident in a dangerous and impersonal superuniverse since Womb Planet had always been so placidly well-ordered. Everything had been in its correct place in their underwater paradise and had always seemed so. It had been perfection; its primal purity preserved by countless generations of Helianx convinced of their good fortune; a complacency that had only become more firmly reinforced after they had seen the tumultuous physical challenges faced by the intelligent species on most of the worlds they had observed astrally. From the security of their waterworld, it had never once occurred to the Helianx that some cosmic intelligence beyond their understanding might have some future plans for them.

Having finally come to terms with the emotional impact of their collective trauma, the last thing the Helianx wanted to believe was that there was some sort of hyper-physical entity, who clearly seemed to have a rather poor opinion of them.

Having conducted a
universe-wide scan of
planetary life-forms, their
computers finally punched
out the co-ordinates of a
small, but marvelously
blue/green, world
somewhat off the general
star routes.
The uniscan
revealed the third and only
inhabited planet of a G3 star,
soon to enter its fourth epoch
of socialization; the first
three having been
destroyed by natural
global disturbances.

But, most importantly,
this strange new world, so
the computers informed
the Helianx, was prime
for a little cohabitation...

Since the Helianx had come late to externalized technology they tended to create what they needed as they needed it: Creation as a direct response to necessity was how they would have contrasted themselves to those more purely technological societies that seemed to have a gadget for everything. The Space Gypsies also had the luxury to observe, in their extensive travels through both the inner and outer worlds of the superuniverse, how different species handled their relationship to technology. Watching some planetary cultures struggling with the consequences of thousands of years of unchecked technological advances, had served to remind the Helianx of their decision to ensure that any creation of theirs would have to remain well within their control.

Having successfully fashioned the Great Ship as their only possible response to the impending planetary disaster, the Helianx became more confident in their ability to construct and materialize *thoughtforms*. This served them well as they settled into a very different life from the one that had been so peaceful back on Womb Planet. They were still careful to respond only to a real need, but their nomadic existence had made new demands on their technical ingenuity. The creation of localized transporters, for example, so necessary for teleporting up the ambassadors and diplomats of the races they had come to know, had led naturally to the desire for more efficient translating devices.

The need for the *Uniscan* had emerged when the Helianx had stumbled upon inhabited worlds they had not previously discovered. While they were orbiting the planet of interest the Uniscan let them see the level of intellectual and spiritual development of the various intelligent species. This had allowed them to avoid belligerent and fearful races and had much simplified their analysis of belief systems. Without having to interact directly they were able to observe, on the enormous screens of the Uniscan, the perennial struggle for survival that dominated life on more primitive worlds. Having had no experience of predation back on Womb Planet, the Helianx found themselves particularly fascinated to watch the long process by which true intelligence climbed out of the instinctual drives that governed the animal nature.

They had to steel themselves from time to time while they looked on in horror, as different species fought each other to extinction, only to frequently destroy themselves, along with their planet, when they finally gained dominance. The endlessly long lifespan of the Helianx frequently gave them the dubious opportunity to watch this entire sorry process reveal itself in realtime on their uniscan screens.

As this long last journey had played itself out, the Helianx realized with a growing sense of foreboding that their computers were urging them to take careful note of the most problematic and challenging biospheres they were encountering - and moreover - to pay particular attention to the emotional and psychological makeup of those beings who survived their brutal evolutionary rise to power.

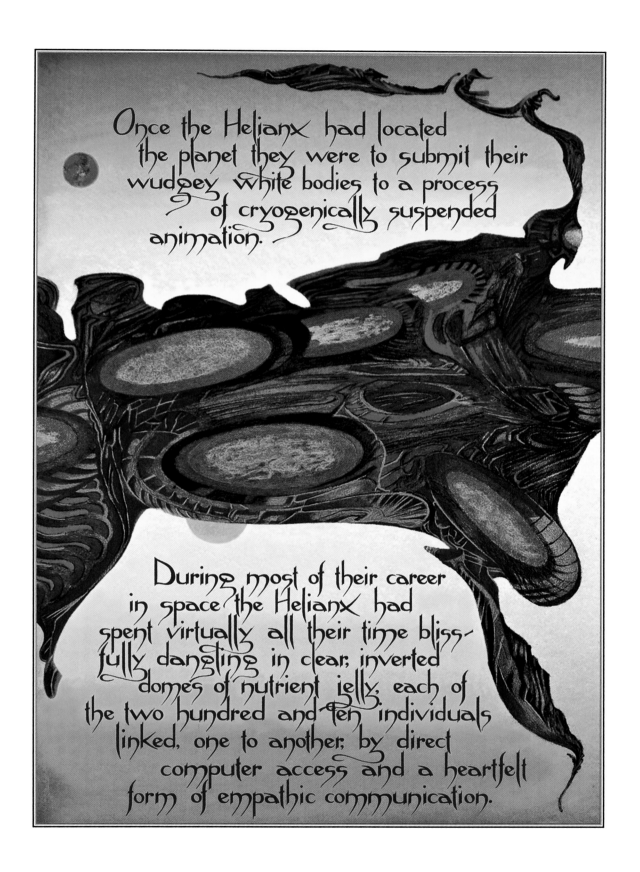

Once the Helianx had located
the planet they were to submit their
wudgey white bodies to a process
of cryogenically suspended
animation.

During most of their career
in space the Helianx had
spent virtually all their time bliss-
fully dangling in clear, inverted
domes of nutrient jelly, each of
the two hundred and ten individuals
linked, one to another, by direct
computer access and a heartfelt
form of empathic communication.

It had taken a long time for the Helianx to get used to life aboard the Great Ship. Although they had taken care to fashion the enormous craft, as far as they could, to emulate conditions on Womb Planet, clearly they were not able to duplicate the size of their destroyed world. This had led to a growing frustration, especially amongst the younger of the surviving Helianx who still carried memories of swimming freely in the pellucid waters of their home planet. As part of the design process their computers had suggested incorporating a series of vast interior spaces, buried in the hold of the ship and filled with water, which would allow the Helianx a chance to exercise their bodies.

However, and this had been quite shocking to the Elders, the computers had insisted on the inclusion of dry chambers representing the planet after the seas had receded. The horror of their recent experience had colored their emotions so deeply that it became as a consequence, an unsung taboo, never to visit, or raise in discussion, the arid, storm-blown simulacrum lodged deep within the bowels of the ship. It was doubtless this impulse that had also led to their gradual acceptance of a more sedentary existence spent largely in the nutrient domes, and of the many obvious restrictions imposed by a peripatetic life in interstellar space.

Galactic historians have stressed the need to understand the enormous time-spans involved when studying these strange creatures. It has always been hard for short-lived entities to grasp the psychological mindset of beings whose long lives could best be expressed in geological time. Do their thoughts move more slowly through those vast neural networks? Do their immensely long life-spans allow them to view universal philosophical questions in a profoundly different way? What meaning does death hold for creatures who die so infrequently? How is time considered, when there is so much of it?

The changes the Helianx underwent as a species occurred over millions of years and many generations of life on the Great Ship. Much of their placid lives had been spent floating in *Dreamtime*, and by the time the computers started spitting out their new prediction for the demise of the superuniverse, the frightful memories of their unfortunate exile had all but dissipated. They had even grown to enjoy the indolence imposed on them by circumstances, broken only by occasional meetings with diplomatic missions, who often seemed unreasonably resentful of the Helianx for the news they brought.

As a result of the increasingly skeptical animosity amongst those they were merely trying to warn, the news that the Helianx were to place themselves in suspended animation for an undetermined period in the future, became a considerably more attractive prospect than might have been anticipated by a more restless species.

Even the computers' tentatively hopeful assurance concerning the life-support systems did little to dampen down their enthusiasm. When the Helianx had considered that this plan might give them a chance to survive, it had seemed a small price to pay.

They were reassured by their computers
that all life-support systems could be
maintained "almost" indefinitely, and
a new form of electronic telementation was
recommended as a bonding mechanism for
this long – and who really knew how long,
period of hibernation.

There was one catch, however. . .

In spite of their size the Helianx could never be thought of as a hardy species. In those early years of the Multiverse, the organic molecules that are the building blocks of life, were made up of a finer substance than those in these more recent and denser times. The computers had been more than aware of this structural frailty and it had been this that had led inevitably to a solution which had to take this factor into account.

When the computers finally revealed the audacious plan they had concocted, the Helianx were forced to confront the sad truth of what had become of their physical condition. They had become so entranced by the languorous pleasures of nil-gravity space, and by this point in time, were arguably so addicted to spending longer and longer periods roaming the out-of-the-body realms, that they had come to place a decreasing importance on their physical bodies. As with most aquatic species, the density of the medium in which they exist tends to blur the borderline between their bodies and their surrounding environment. It becomes increasingly difficult for them to pay attention to where their bodies end and where the water starts. If such a creature evolves without having to deal with the constant presence of predatory enemies, there is little to prevent it from spending almost all its time free of its body, traveling the subtle dimensions of the Multiverse.

The planetary catastrophe had been the first severe awakening for the Helianx and they had done their best in those early years on the Great Ship to make sure to keep their bodies toned up and physically strong. But, as the millennia passed and their confidence in the space glider grew to a point at which they could engage the autopilot for long periods of time, they reverted gradually to their old ways. They floated free in the astral realms, their enormous, amorphous bodies curled and furled in the security of the nutrient domes. It had been a stern reminder for the Helianx to realize, in the light of harsh cosmic realities, just how physically weakened they had allowed themselves to become.

The fact that the plan the computers had evolved was centrally dependent on one individual Helianx was also of particular concern to the Elders, since in the course of their entire history the Helianx had never been truly separated. The bonding that resulted from their telepathic group-mind tended to de-emphasize their individuality, and when they chose to travel out-of-the-body they preferred to move as one collective identity. Relying for their species continuing existence on any one single individual, however, seemed to them to be the height of folly. Many of the Elders had strongly resisted the whole idea, until the computers had demonstrated unequivocally that in spite of the obvious risks there was no other way they would have a chance of ultimate survival.

The Helianx understood they were going to have to resign themselves to the hard choice, hope for the best, and trust in the wisdom of their computers to have calculated the odds in their favor.

Since the generally weakened state of the Helianx had taken its toll on the life-energy of their race, their computers predicated the success of the venture on the pooling of this pranic energy into a single entity.

It was the fate of the one being to be placed on the planet of choice and to mingle with the natives, as it were, until such time as this individual Helianx – whatever its physical form was to become – would return to the great, silent ship, and reactivate its dormant denizens.

There were other catches too, but those our intrepid centipede would not learn until later.

The Great Ship, wafting at near-light speedy on glistening gossamer sails one million miles across, took half-an-aeon to reach its calculated destination.

Inside the ship, preparations were getting underway for the day of final refloration.

The Great Ship was a marvel of bioplasmic engineering. Since the Helianx had originally created their computers by seeding a bioelectronic matrix with their own protoplasm, so also had the computers, in their turn, recommended the same process in the creation of the spaceship. This had allowed the Helianx to mold the craft to their precise specifications in an organic material with which they felt a natural resonance.

It was their familiarity with the *ultimatonic* structure of matter that had originally alerted the Helianx to the intelligence lodged within it, and which, in turn, led them to their mastery over the manipulation of matter. Although they did not fully understand the processes concerned, the intimacy of their involvement with the molding of molecules drawn initially from their own bodies had led them to a much deeper recognition of the inherent sentience in matter. The nature of the intelligence they had discovered was so different from anything they had previously encountered; so diffuse and subtle, so caring in nature and yet so vastly indifferent to the savagery of cosmic collisions, that they could well appreciate how its presence had been overlooked by them for so long.

What the Helianx found in their explorations into the core of matter had revolutionized the way they had thought about the Creation. It was knowing about this fundamental sentience that had allowed them to work collaboratively with it, accomplishing tasks they would not have considered possible before the planetary calamity forced them to face up to the impending disaster. They had been able to micromanage the molecular structure of their own bodies for as long as any one of them could remember, fashioning the simple tools they needed for their underwater life. But the intense pressure to design and build the ship had necessitated a profound deepening in their intuitive grasp of the inherent desire in matter to become form.

As a sculptress might gaze at a slab of marble to discover the form buried within its structure, so also had the Helianx, by cooperating with the subtle whispers they were receiving from the Heart of Matter, sculpted the living protoplasm into the organic structure of the Great Ship. And because it became a living thing, the craft responded autonomously to the needs of the moment. Elegantly surfing the gravity waves, the ship took it upon itself to grow great sails that gathered the cosmic winds and transduced the energy into a propulsive force, capable of accelerating the enormous vehicle to breathtaking speeds.

When the Helianx were approaching an inhabited galaxy the sensitive sails intuitively reversed the energy flow, slowing the ship down and locking it into a convenient orbit around the planet of interest. At that point the sails, ever-respondant to what was required of them, would furl themselves around and behind the body of the ship, so as to appear to those on the planet, like the distant glimmer of a comet slowly circling their world.

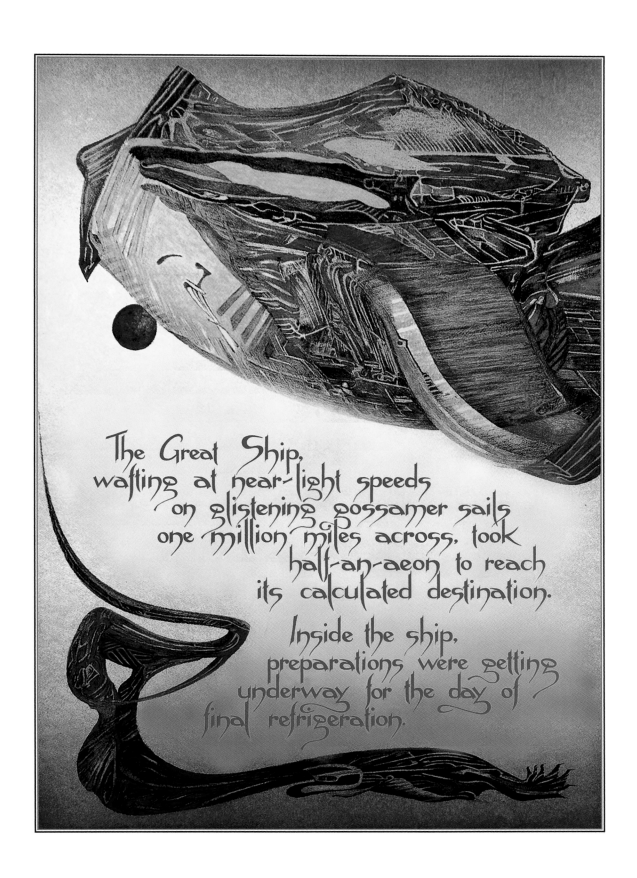

The Great Ship,
wafting at near-light speeds
on glistening gossamer sails
one million miles across, took
half-an-aeon to reach
its calculated destination.

Inside the ship,
preparations were getting
underway for the day of
final refrigeration.

A series of meetings were held among the Council of Elders to decide which of the Helianx would have the doubtful pleasure of a plummeting fall through time.

Finally the omniscient computers, once again came to their rescue reducing the list to one—a highly individualistic poet who went by the name of *Nilx*.

Since the Helianx had traditionally maintained their population at the relatively small number of 210, and compounded by their immensely long life-spans, the bonding they experienced as a race was so intimate and interdependent that the prospect of being separated from any one of their number was perhaps the most difficult challenge they had had to face up to this point.

As the horrors of their planetary exodus, so many millions of years earlier, dimmed in their collective memory, the Helianx had tended to fall back into their old, easygoing ways of life on Womb Planet. Their explorations of the superuniverse had proved it to be essentially unthreatening. The few belligerent races they had encountered sensibly avoided any confrontation with the mountainous Space Gypsies. Despite the speeds attainable by the Great Ship, the vastness of the interstellar distances ensured that the Helianx spent much of their time passively suspended in a collective meditational trance, broken only when the ship was placed securely in geosynchronous orbit around one of the planets they were studying. Then, emerging reluctantly from the warm embrace of Oneness, they would individuate sufficiently to entertain the visiting diplomats and ambassadors in the reception chambers of the enormous glider.

The Helianx had learned enough about the nature of the Multiverse by this time to understand how the seven superuniverses were enfolded within the seven primary dimensions of the Multiverse. Those more metaphysically minded had even started to invoke the need for the existence of a *Central Universe* that lay behind, or, as some suggested, within the very heart of the spacetime continuum. They understood also that this Central Universe acted as a pattern creation for the seven subsequent superuniverses. As the Multiverse aged and the inhabited worlds of the subsequent superuniverses became settled in *Light and Life,* the vibrational frequency of matter itself slowed down and grew denser. Consequently, all the species created and seeded throughout the seventh of these superuniverses were formed of a considerably denser material than the creatures existing in the earlier creations.

It was this very factor that the computers counseled might be turned to the Space Gypsies' advantage in the matter of their ultimate survival. For the Helianx to accomplish their purpose they knew they would have to project the one chosen by their computers on what was essentially a journey down through the spacetime continuum, to arrive, hopefully, on a world somewhere in the seventh and final superuniverse.

They had little idea of what this individual Helianx would find when sHe finally arrived on the designated planet, but they suspected that it was going to be a lot more demanding than anything they had previously experienced. It was also next to impossible for the Council of Elders to imagine how the denser medium of the seventh superuniverse would affect the emotional intelligence of the beings inhabiting it. But here again, their computers had reassured them that the challenges would only serve to strengthen the emotional muscles of the Helianx for the demanding tasks that lay ahead of hir.

A series of meetings were held among
the Council of Elders to decide
which of the Helianx would have the
doubtful pleasure of a plummeting
fall through time.

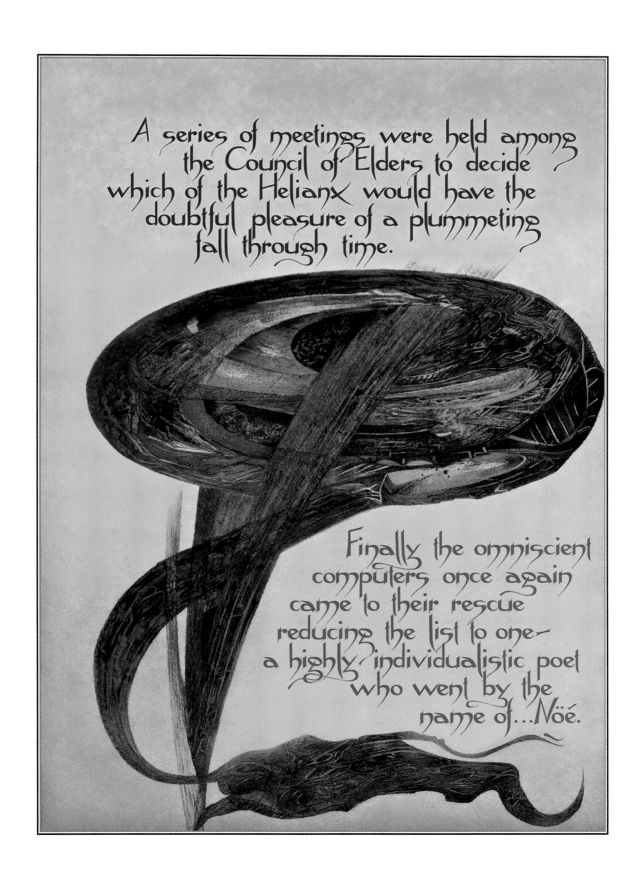

Finally the omniscient
computers once again
came to their rescue
reducing the list to one—
a highly individualistic poet
who went by the
name of...Nöé.

The Council of Elders had debated long into the galactic night as to which of their race would have to carry this heavy responsibility. Everything would have to ultimately depend on this single being. A minority of the Council had recommended choosing one of their own number since the depth of an Elder's experience would prove to be invaluable in what they could only imagine would be a thoroughly hostile environment. Others had felt that a younger, more flexible mind would be better able to deal with the inevitable unpredictability of life at that late stage of Multiverse development.

The Helianx had never considered themselves to be an unreasonably courageous race. Long ago, the terrified survivors had managed to drag themselves off their planet by dint of intelligence and determination, but it had not made them particularly brave. As the Elders contemplated what might be required of the chosen Helianx, they realized just how little they knew about the evolution of intelligent life on planets as young and primitive as the one chosen for them by their computers.

The Uniscan had allowed them to peer through the mists of time to scan and locate the planet in the first place, but the device's limitations had prevented them from seeing all but a very narrow slice of the previous planet's history. Their many journeys in the *astral realms* had been restricted to the inhabited planets of the early superuniverses, so they had little or no data on the condition of life in the seventh.

As has been previously noted, travel between the second and seventh superuniverse had never even been considered prior to the point that the Helianx speculated about the possibility of lowering their vibrational frequency sufficiently to interact with the material reality of the seventh superuniverse. They all knew it was going to be a high-risk operation and that they had to get it right first time around with no real practice beforehand. Until then, the whole plan had to remain a theory, a mere speculation upon which their very survival would have to depend.

Galactic historians have never been able to find any evidence of travel by other races between fundamentally different dimensions, but since the Helianx presence has only recently been revealed, the academics have had to resume their search for hints that others indeed may have made the same improbable leap, and have since managed to keep it a secret.

Meanwhile, there is a general agreement in the more forward-looking of the great *Melchizedek Universities*, that when the seventh superuniverse becomes more advanced and settled in Light and Life, there will be a lifting of the veils that separate the different dimensions. They speculate that all created beings in the seven superuniverses will finally have free access to one another. Then, as the secrets of the ages drop away, they believe that the Living Multiverse will reveal itself in all its coherent Oneness, and a new Supreme purpose will emerge, giving a yet deeper meaning to the existence of all life.

Being quite
naturally
biased to-
wards music
and epic poetry they were happy,
but still a little surprised, that
the choice led to this particular
young and outspoken
Helianx,
known for Hir
adventurous spirit
and too-smart-
by-half
ways.

But,
by this time, the tidal
stresses of the wrench to
come were starting
to take their toll on
the sensitive
body
Helianx

Our poet was hurriedly recalled from an indefinite sabbatical in some far-flung corner of the vast ship. Terra-formed within seemingly endless spherical boundaries into a vague but romanticized reminder of Womb Planet.

The closeness of the bonding the Helianx experienced as a race had deepened considerably in their long last swing through the inhabited worlds of the second superuniverse.

It was toward the end of their altruistic mission that the Elders had noticed gradual, but radical, changes taking place in some of the younger Helianx. Nöé, for example, had taken to spending an increasing amount of time on hir own, appearing to explore the vast interior spaces of the Great Ship. Some of hir younger contemporaries were also showing signs of individuation such that the Elders had not seen since the dreadful years when the biosphere on Womb Planet was collapsing. Yet that phase had been driven by fear while these puzzling new changes appeared to have no immediate cause.

As the realization had sunk in that their oceans really were evaporating, the frightening impact had temporarily fractured the fragile consciousness of the youngest of the Helianx. Curling in on themselves in fear, they had found themselves disconnected from the Web for the first time and had panicked, wildly swimming off in different directions. It had taken acts of unprecedented self-discipline by the Elders to stabilize the Web and to draw the youngsters back into the relative safety of the collective consciousness of the group. It was only then that the Helianx had found it possible to gather sufficient pranic energy to fashion the space glider and they had not quickly forgotten the lesson.

This bitter memory directly contributed to the Elders' initial nervousness when they observed Nöé's evident desire to spend so much time on hir own. They finally relaxed somewhat on seeing that sHe seemed to be fearless in hir solo explorations and genuinely curious to simulate the lives of the many species represented in the ship's holographic museum. Using a subsystem of the acoustic holography that their computers had developed as an aid to storing the immense amount of information gathered, the Helianx had designed selected chambers in the ship to act as 3D platforms for massive holograms of the living environment of the worlds they had visited.

These exhibits were designed in collaboration with their computers to be participatory holograms, cunningly activated by the songs they had gathered and synthesized. By relaying the songs in a specific sequence the explorer could energize the hologram to cycle through the important events in the evolution of that particular race; all their achievements and challenges, their artistic and scientific accomplishments; their hopes and fears; and, most important to the Helianx, the belief systems that the race had constructed to explain the Creation to themselves.

In this way the young Helianx were able to have an experiential taste of the worlds their forebears had visited, and at the same time had a compelling and beguiling reason to learn their songs and mythic histories. In fact, a visit to the holographic museum in the company of one of the more experienced Helianx quickly became the high point of the shipboard meetings for the alien diplomats teleported up to the Great Ship.

Our poet was hurriedly recalled
from an indefinite sabbatical in some
far-flung corner of the vast ship,
terra-formed within seemingly
endless spherical boundaries into a
vague, but romanticized reminder
of Womb Planet.

Nöé, our poet, had been located finally in Hir clear plastic-standard hour-research craft, drifting idly over the interminable yellow sands, singing songs of desolation and rebirth.

In Hir favor the Elders noted the poet had the unlikely habit of settling the craft down onto the surface. SHe would lever Hirself gently out onto the soft sand and flex Hir by-now almost entirely atrophied little legs, happily flouting the one and only fixed taboo of a decadently permissive race—that of any involvement with matters gravitational.

When the Helianx designed the Great Ship, their computers had insisted on including a large simulacrum of Womb Planet to be buried deep within the hold of the craft. This was not to be a mere hologram, but needed to be fabricated directly into the structure of the ship. The Helianx had been advised to fashion their substitute world as a simulation of their planet at the point at which there were still large lakes separated by dry and sandy mesas. The computers had wanted to duplicate the most challenging environment the Helianx had had to face in those dreadful last years. But they had relented slightly when the Elders had suggested that it would be far more valuable to include a wider range of physical conditions. They had maintained that in this manner the younger Helianx--born after their world had been destroyed--would have some idea of what it was like to swim in the constricted and diminishing waters of their home planet.

In their omnisentient wisdom, the computers had understood that it was important for the Helianx to have a sentimental remembrance of the glorious days before the nova. Although the compromise reached did not completely satisfy either party, the spacious lakes had allowed the Elders to initiate the young ones into an admittedly vague reminder of what life had been like in an increasingly distant past.

In retrospect, we can now appreciate that even in those early stages of shipbuilding, and well before they had finished crunching the numbers on the many cosmologies they had collected, the computers had been starting judiciously to prepare the Helianx for the trials ahead. Later, the Elders were grateful for this fortunate prescience. However, they still remained profoundly disturbed by the sight of those bleak and barren hills, on the rare occasions they were required to accompany a young initiate to the simulated world in the hold of the ship. The pair would slip into the water-filled tunnels that linked the maze of chambers to the furthest and most private reaches of the craft, where they had located the enormous simulacrum. Without surfacing, the Elder would guide hir young companion directly into the great central lake. Then, by placing hir massive body between the coastline and the sight line of hir younger ward, they were both able conveniently to avoid any thought of those barren, sandy hills, and the frightful memories that the devastated landscape invariably raised.

Planetary *psychohistorians* have since speculated that whilst the Helianx might well have dedicated themselves to investigating the physical and spiritual causes for the demise of their world, they clearly had not come to emotional terms with the trauma. Some have suggested that it was by consistently ignoring the implications of the intense gravitational field and the harsh conditions of the arid desert above the waterline, that the collective consciousness of the Helianx had developed what might be considered a carapace of psychic scar tissue.

Over time, this level of profound denial resulted in a cultural taboo which effectively discouraged all the younger Helianx from exploring the arid wastes. All, apparently, with the exception of Nöé.

Nöé, our poet, had been located
finally in Hir clear plastic-
standard issue-research
craft, drifting idly over
the interminable yellow
sands, singing songs
of desolation and
rebirth.

In Hir favor, the Elders noted,
the poet had the unlikely habit
of settling the craft down
onto the surface.
SHe would lever Hirself gently
out onto the soft sand and flex
Hir by-now almost entirely
atrophied little legs, happily
flouting the one and only fixed
taboo of a decadently permissive race-that of any involvement
with matters gravitational.

Womb Planet, in its past glory, had been one of the largest inhabited planets in the second superuniverse. It had been formed originally from space debris which aggregated around the heavy elements thrown out from the twin suns, as they settled into equilibrium with one another. Originally the two stars had been a single, enormous, solar furnace spun off from a nebular mother wheel, and so large that it had split into two as it cooled and condensed. It was during this cosmic mitosis that explosive forces threw off sheets of semi-gaseous matter which slowly condensed into what was to become Womb Planet.

Due to its odd figure-of-eight orbit around the two neighboring stars, Womb Planet gathered more material than usual, including a large moon. Both bodies grew progressively more massive over time through the accretion of so much of the detritus spewed out by the stellar paroxysm. This had resulted in the unusual arrangement of a binary star system with only one inhabitable planet. Tiny planetoids, and the few captured asteroids not scooped up by Womb Planet's gravitational hunger, circled each of the stars, whilst the planet, alone with its single, lifeless moon, swung through its eccentric orbit around the two maternal stars.

In those early cycles of Multiverse development, when solar systems and their planetary families were being formed, comets were far more plentiful than they are today. As Womb Planet had grown in size and gravitational heft it had attracted comets of every size towards its surface; the melting ice gradually deepening the ocean that ultimately covered the entire world.

Due to its immense size, Womb Planet exerted a gravitational pull estimated to have been at least three times more powerful than one of a more average mass. But, since sentient life had originated in the oceans, as it does on most planets, this mattered little to the nascent life-forms which were to evolve into the creatures that became the Helianx.

Over the millions of years, as the creatures' physiology adapted to the extremes of their aquatic world, their bodies grew in size and gradually developed the ability to withstand the crushing pressure of the ocean in the deepest of the underwater canyons. When disaster had finally struck and they were forced to clamber over the emerging land masses in search of the remaining deep water, the Helianx were relieved to find that their bodies had been somewhat prepared for the unaccustomed weight of gravity. In spite of this, and as the conditions worsened, most of those who expired had found movement so difficult that it had slowed their progress. Dehydrated, they had shriveled and died in the harsh light of their twin suns.

Unlike the majority of inhabited planets, in which the patterns laid into their DNA had been designed to coax a species at the appropriate time out of the water and onto the land, the Helianx had never experienced any such instinctual drive to leave their friendly oceans. It had seemed to the survivors an unfortunate irony that, in their case, it had been the seas that had deserted them.

The simulated three gravities pressure would start to pull on well-nigh forgotten muscles and Nöe's new, small, vestigial wings would flap and slap in the dry, desert winds.

Galactic exobiologists have recently theorized that the principle of using DNA as the fundamental coding for organic life might well hold true throughout all seven superuniverses. Much to the surprise of the scientists, every sentient species so far studied, however morphologically different, has revealed some remarkably similar basic arrangements of nucleotides in their biological makeup.

Their observations also suggest that mutations--which drive evolution on more normally seeded planets--emerge spontaneously when the relevant gene pool reaches a certain size and the physical environment encourages it in some way. However, they had to admit that evolution must have occurred very differently for the Helianx. What then had allowed these creatures to develop to such a degree of complexity given the limited size of their gene pool?

What had been so puzzling for these scientists was to find a race of intelligent beings whose evolutionary path appeared to be so different from the norm. There was even some talk of the possibility that the Helianx, widely known to be fabulists and storytellers, had not arisen as the only species on Womb Planet as they maintained; and further, that originally there had been many more of them in the early history of their world. True or not, this had been the only way these academically trained geneticists could explain the odd improbability that the Helianx represented.

What these critics had not fully appreciated was the precise nature of the relationship between the Helianx and their internal processes. In the many millions of years of aquatic evolution, drifting idly in the warm waters of Womb Planet, the creatures had turned naturally to the slower rhythms of meditation and relaxed self-inspection. Since there had been no predators and little external to themselves to distract them, they were encouraged to spend an increasing amount of time in a light-trance state. It was this inner stillness that had originally allowed them to stumble upon the dimensional portals to the out-of-the-body realms that they were later to travel so extensively.

Of more immediate importance to the introspective Helianx was the astonishing discovery of what they came to think of as their body-devas. At first, these devas had manifested as autonomous, quasi-intelligent, organizing principles which seemed to cohabit with the Helianx somewhere within their enormous bodies. Their function appeared to be to handle the immense amount of electrochemical and biological information that it took to keep the creatures alive and healthy. As contact and communication with their devas deepened, the Space Gypsies slowly came to understand the possibilities that this intimate relationship opened up. With trust building up over time, it was this collaborative alliance that had led to the unprecedented ability of the Helianx to manipulate their own DNA.

When disaster had struck Womb Planet, this profound intimacy became lost in the intense struggle to survive, and their devas, disconnected temporarily from the consciousness of their amiable hosts, had attempted on their own to second-guess what the Helianx might need to secure their continuing survival.

A note: In the course of their millions of years as nil-gravity space wanderers the genetic coding of the Helianx, perplexed at the species dramatic and sudden move into intergalactic space, had responded by digging into their biological repertoire and bestowing small leathery wings upon some of the more advanced amongst them.

When Nöé saw the bone craft skimming over the hills towards Hir SHe sensed Hir training in surface life the young Helianx had garnered in Hir escapades through the terra-formed worlds residing in the bowels of the vast ship was now over...

The Elders noted that one of the unusual aspects of Nöé's sly expeditions into the simulated desert in the hold of the Great Ship, was the enthusiastic way in which the young Helianx disconnected hirself from the constant telepathic chatter of the Web. As with most telepathic species, the Helianx could always act a trifle skittish around the subject of individuation. It had not come naturally to them. The planetary trauma, while it was still echoing in the group mind, had served to discourage all but the youngest amongst them from exploring what it meant to be a singular being.

The Elders would weave their great heads from side to side in gestures of mutual puzzlement, half-horrified and half-fascinated by Nöé's seemingly irrational behavior. This concern was only compounded by hir newfound ability to block the Elders' telepathic probings when sHe returned finally from hir lengthy and mysterious visits to the arid desert hidden away in the hold. Being intensely inquisitive by nature, a curiosity fueled by their appreciation of the limitless variety of life forms they had encountered in their journeys, the Elders could only suppress their frustrations in the light of Nöé's evident recalcitrance.

The truth of this, however, was rather more straightforward than the Elders might have imagined. Nöé had no idea either of quite why sHe was being drawn so consistently back to the inhospitable wastes. SHe had decided simply to follow hir intuition, or what sHe had come to think of as the clearest of hir inner voices. This development was something new to hir and had only started to manifest as sHe had progressively detached from the easy familiarity of the Web and its constant distractions.

Nöé, like all adolescent Helianx, had been taught from infancy about their race's discovery of the intelligence inherent in matter, and how that knowledge had been so vital in allowing the Helianx to fashion their biological artifacts. SHe learned for hirself, along with the other young ones and through much trial and error, how to tickle out the intentions coded into matter on an *ultimatonic* level; and how to work collaboratively with the apparent proclivity of matter to settle into the natural forms the Helianx observed all around them. SHe knew, too, how this insight had come to form the basis of their understanding of astrophysics. Research consistently revealed that a primal organizing intelligence, working through matter at its most basic level, was actively shaping the spacetime continuum. How else, they reasoned, had the stars become stars; how had their families of planets been created in all their wonderful variety and, above all, why had so many of these worlds turned out to be so ideally suited for the evolution of organic, sentient life? The Helianx all agreed that there had to be a fundamental purpose to Creation.

What they had not yet deduced, in spite of their extensive travels through the astral planes, was what they came much later to understand as the celestial realms. At this point in time, and throughout the many millennia of the Helianx diaspora, the intelligent organizing principles, those whose hidden hands lay behind the material universes, had continued to remain a complete mystery to them.

When Nöé saw the base craft skimming over the hills towards Hir. SHe sensed Hir sabbatical was over. Whatever training in surface life the young Helianx had garnered in Hir escapades through the terra-formed worlds nestling in the bowels of the vast ship was now over...

And, in a profound way, a new journey was soon to start.

When Nöé first became aware of hir inner voices sHe was both puzzled and confused. SHe wondered whether sHe was losing hir senses. It seemed to occur solely when sHe had detached hirself from the Web and sHe only did that in hir visits to the hold of the Great Ship. SHe had tried to discuss this unusual manifestation with the Elders, but was invariably met with blank incomprehension. It soon became clear to Nöé that none of hir companions had experienced anything quite like this. After a few frustrating attempts to describe this ephemeral phenomena, sHe decided sensibly to keep what was happening to hirself.

What had originally been so perplexing to Nöé was the manner in which these inner voices had whispered to hir spontaneously and so completely unbidden. One of the voices, however, was quite different from the rest. When it had started this voice had seemed to Nöé to be so close to hir own intuition that sHe found it almost impossible to separate it from hir own deepest feelings and desires. Unlike the communication matrix which had developed into the Web, this voice was, quite literally, a Voice, and not the customary sonic holograms so familiar to all Helianx.

Nöé was acutely aware that their computers had been laboring long into the galactic night to try to find a solution to the problem of their race's survival. Having been thoroughly trained in the subtle arts of ultimatonic modulation, sHe knew what a lengthy and complex operation this entailed.

As with many intelligent aquatic species, the Helianx had discovered over the course of their evolution that their soundings could be modulated to carry visual images that would flicker on the *eidetic screen* of their inner eyes. Over time, this led naturally to their ability to manipulate matter according to a design held in their collective imagination. In addition to the clarity of intention needed to shape matter into the required form--for example, the small, robotic base craft that was even now skimming over the windswept sands to fetch hir--Nöé knew that it had taken a minimum of ten Helianx to create it. This group had to be prepared to hold a focused meditation for the length of time it took to *psychokinetically* rearrange the organic molecules into the desired structure.

This process was psychically and physically exhausting and had ultimately discouraged the Helianx from using their mental powers for anything not absolutely essential to their survival; the sole exception being in service of their obsessive anthropological research expeditions. So, when Nöé saw the base craft sHe could appreciate the effort that must have gone into manifesting it. And this, coupled with the quiet but insistent counsel of the Inner Voice, convinced hir that the computers must have found their answer.

In spite of Nöé's idiosyncratic behavior, as odd to hir as it was to the Elders, and the gentle prompting of this strange and unexpected Voice, sHe had no real idea of what lay ahead, or the destiny that awaited hir. But, as sHe heaved hir bulky body into the cramped interior of the base craft, Nöé could not help wondering whether all these events were in some way connected.

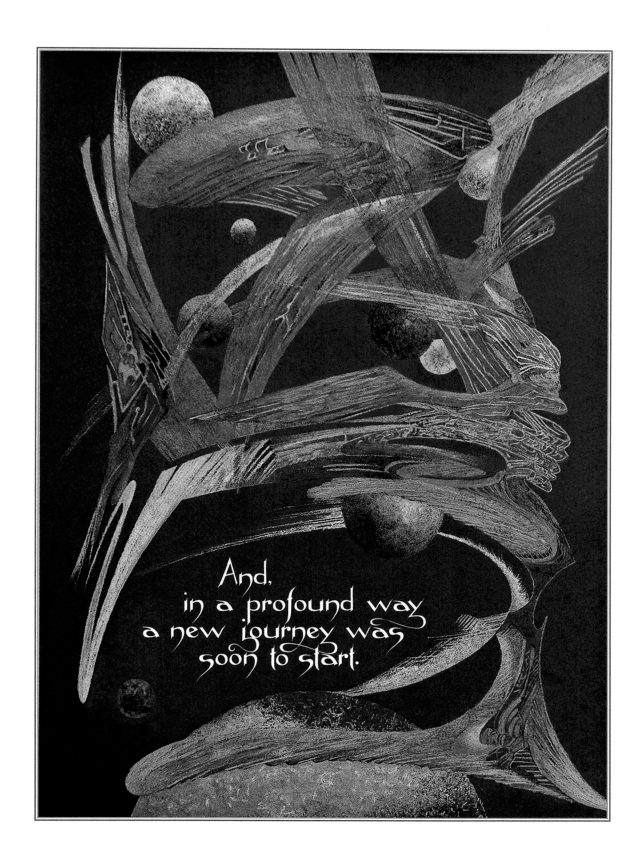

And,
in a profound way
a new journey was
soon to start.

Back at the Hub the ensuing computer briefing, short though it was, made the central point loud and clear. With very little practice beforehand Nöe was to have one full unimpeded shot at co-opting the collaboration of the indigenous dominant life-forms before the stresses of gravity would tear apart the massive white soft body of the Helianx.

Admittedly, all was not then completely lost since...

The base craft was able to reach the Hub far more rapidly than Nöé could have by swimming through the maze of interconnecting corridors stretching throughout the hold of the Great Ship. SHe had not greeted its arrival with much pleasure since sHe had planned for one of hir more extensive stays on the sandy plains of the simulated desert, and had decided to return to the comfort of the Hub and the companionship of the others only when sHe could no longer stand the stresses of life on dry land.

Being by nature a somewhat indolent species, even Nöé had been originally perplexed by the newfound inner Voice's gentle insistence on spending longer and longer periods on hir own in this thoroughly inhospitable environment. But, as sHe became more accustomed to the rigors of surface life, sHe started to realize that sHe might be being prepared for whatever lay ahead.

The computers had taken far longer than the Helianx anticipated for a thorough analysis of the possibilities facing their species. It was one thing to gain an understanding of the physical properties of matter, and how it was arranged on both the microcosmic and macrocosmic levels, but quite another to try to outwit the very forces that threatened to destroy them. It was always going to be a gamble and the long wait had only served to reinforce their fears that there might be, in fact, no solution whatsoever to this most pressing of problems. This was clearly not a straightforward project and they knew it would challenge their computers to the very limit of their prescient powers.

Had they been a younger and simpler race, or perhaps more fatalistic by nature, the Helianx might have resigned themselves to their extinction, as had some of the other species on the worlds they had visited, having allowed their technology to spin out of control. The Helianx had to remind themselves that they had been in this situation before, and they had managed to avoid extinction by dint of pushing both their computers, and themselves, to new and previously inconceivable heights of imagination. Even the most conservative amongst them had to admit that they never would have been able to contemplate their move into space without the farsighted collaboration of their computers.

As with most telepathic species, the Helianx had always tended to think of themselves as a psychic and spiritual Oneness, as a singularity dominated by the intimacy of the Web. Indeed, it was this deep sense of homogeneity that most likely inflated their shocked reaction to the plan the computers had evolved. Not only did the stratagem demand that they place their confidence in only one of their race, but it appeared that the computers had already chosen the most unlikely candidate.

Nöé's recent activities, hir apparent indifference to the most sacred of their taboos, and hir insistence on breaking free of the Web, had not endeared hir to the Elders. What even the wisest of them could never have fully appreciated at that time was that Nöé, alone amongst them all, had developed the rare taste for a much more solitary life.

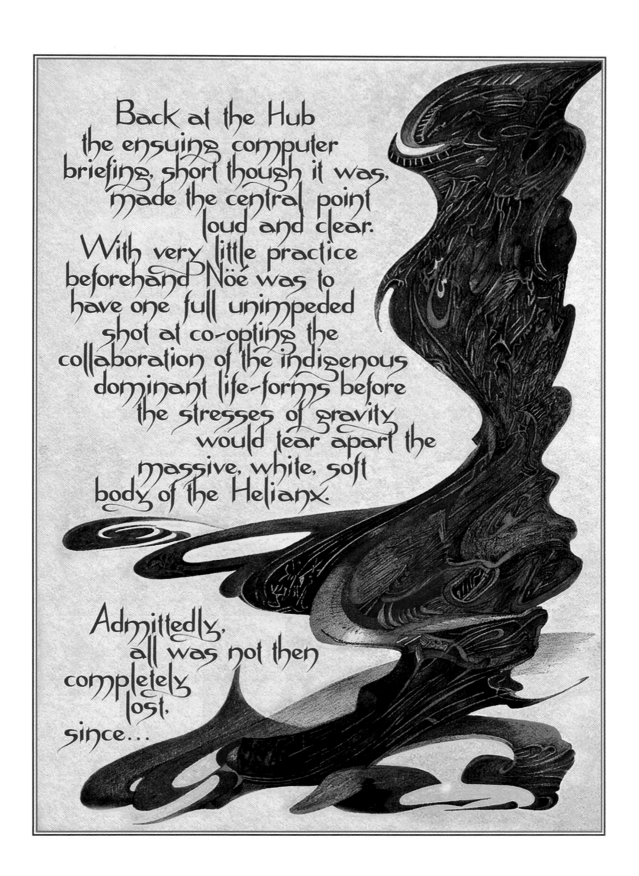

Back at the Hub
the ensuing computer
briefing, short though it was,
made the central point
loud and clear.
With very little practice
beforehand Nöé was to
have one full unimpeded
shot at co-opting the
collaboration of the indigenous
dominant life-forms before
the stresses of gravity
would tear apart the
massive, white, soft
body of the Helianx.

Admittedly,
all was not then
completely
lost,
since...

the life span of the Helianx
had become virtually limitless
and the principle of essence
reincarnation, common in nearly
all sentient species, still held true.

Nice to know,
but of no immediate help,
since without the memory banks
of the shipboard computers and the
continuing knowledge stream
of the Helianic culture, everything
Nöe knew at the time would
be promptly forgotten
upon Hir physical
death.

In spite of their computers' remarkable powers, the Helianx were more than aware that their bioelectronic associates were not soothsayers. They did not see visions or make vague prophesies in the manner of so many of the clairvoyants and prophets they had encountered in their planetary studies. The Helianx well knew that the best the computers would ever be able to deliver was only based on extrapolations derived from data collected over their long career as space wanderers.

As an example of this, they would remind themselves of the days in the far past when they had first observed the red-shift in distant stars and had erroneously deduced that the Multiverse was expanding. How little they had known about the true nature of Reality at that stage. It had taken the computers' diligent and lengthy analysis to persuade them that they were only seeing half the picture. Think of it as breathing, the computers had suggested. Consider the Multiverse as a finite living being floating in a sea of infinity. Searching their data banks for an appropriate metaphor, they added that it was like an unimaginably large, toroidal jelly fish--and the Helianx knew all about jelly fish--pulsating in great slow waves, compressing and expanding, in and out, in and out, and yet always retaining essentially the same form.

Picture yourselves, the computers had continued, in one of the seven superuniverses distributed evenly over the surface and throughout the volume of this enormously large creature. These superuniverses are divided into numerous smaller sectors called *Local Universes*, each one capable of supporting ten million inhabited planets. Imagine, now, looking across the surface, out towards the distant galaxies, while the Multiverse is in its out-breath, the stars will appear to be moving away from you. In another Multiverse era, when the in-breath is the dominant respiration, you will perceive a blue-shift as the distant stars speed towards you. The computers added that the clockwise motion of the Multiverse, as it circles the Central Universe, can also create the illusion of expansion since the first of the far-distant *outer space levels* is spinning in the opposite, anti-clockwise, direction--thus accelerating the illusion and creating much confusion.

Until the Helianx had discovered, as a result of their travels, the subtle hints of the existence of another cluster of galaxies in quite another superuniverse, the tremendous distances and the inherent curvature of the spacetime continuum had prevented their astronomers from becoming aware of the other six superuniverses. And they knew nothing at all about the outer space levels. This knowledge had come much later. At that point in time the Helianx were still coming to terms with the implications of the actions that their computers had recommended as the only possible resolution. Although originally designed to help codify their extensive researches into the cultural, religious and philosophical belief systems of the many worlds the Helianx had visited, and perhaps provoked further by the computers' invaluable contribution to the design of their craft, the Helianx had by now developed a somewhat ambivalent attitude toward their technology. After the initial shock at the choice of Nöe had worn off, the Elders even found it necessary to reassure the others that their virtually omniscient computers had proved reliable enough in the past, perhaps the best strategy would be to trust them one more time.

...the life span of the Helianx
had become virtually limitless
and the principle of essence
reincarnation, common in nearly
all sentient species, still held true.

Nice to know,
but of no immediate help,
since without the memory banks
of the shipboard computers and the
continuing knowledge stream
of the Helianx culture, everything
Nöe knew at the time would
be promptly forgotten
upon Hir physical
death.

The basic biology of the Helianx has remained something of a mystery to latter-day planetary scientists. Quite how life evolved in the early superuniverses has never been fully understood, since little evidence remains of the species created so many millions of years ago. That the Helianx were masters of their own biological processes is clear from the instructions laid out for Nöé by the computers; but the concept that sHe was to meld hir DNA with another species entirely was something the Helianx had never explored, or even seriously considered.

It is thought that in those early days of Creation, the *Beings of the Inner Worlds,* whose function it was to design and lay down the patterns of evolutionary life, were experimenting with some very different reproductive strategies. The essentially hermaphroditic nature of the Helianx, in the sense that each creature was capable of expressing both male and female procreative organs, had allowed them a wide measure of control over their biological destiny.

Over time, and through their studied practice of *Eugenics,* the Helianx had found that there had been periods in their development when it had been appropriate to procreate by a more normal mixing of chromosomes that results from the sexual coupling of two, or more, creatures. Once they had stabilized their population, their preferred method of reproduction became internal insemination, a form of procreation they thought of as auto-cloning. While this had somewhat reduced the genetic diversity, they observed that the young ones delivered in this way possessed the more finely developed psychic sensitivities required for *serial reincarnation.* It was also through this spiritual process that the Helianx had first been able to create their telepathic Web, which subsequently became so central to their lives.

Planetary Anthropologists of the Sacred have recently suggested that serial reincarnation was more widely practiced in the earlier eras in the evolution of intelligent life. This had the evident advantage of producing extremely conservative cultures, which then served to stabilize the gradual growth of sentience in the universes of time and space. The downside, however, which the Helianx had the cosmic misfortune to experience so directly, was that this very conservatism had ill-prepared them for the disaster facing their world. The stability that had served them so well for many millions of years in their underwater world suddenly held no value for them. A growing panic had rippled endlessly through the Web, making it almost impossible for any of them to focus on what was happening to them. They had lost almost three-quarters of their number in the global catastrophe and the survivors, those who had supported the stringent eugenics, had blamed themselves for so slavishly following the traditions of their ancestors. This bruising realization had led them to ensure that they would rebuild their genetic diversity when they were safely established on the Great Ship.

Since Nöé was amongst the younger Helianx to be born on the Great Ship, it was fortunate for hir future mission that sHe had made hirself familiar with the process of serial reincarnation. It would be the only way in which sHe would be able to maintain a continuity of the Helianx knowledge stream over hir long exile on the planet of choice.

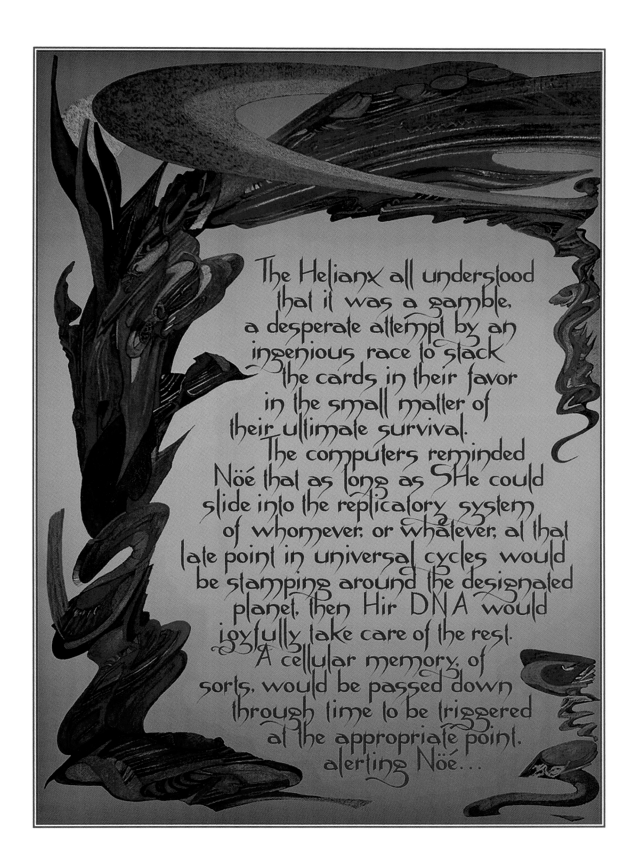

The Helianx all understood
that it was a gamble,
a desperate attempt by an
ingenious race to stack
the cards in their favor
in the small matter of
their ultimate survival.
The computers reminded
Nöé that as long as SHe could
slide into the replicatory system
of whomever, or whatever, at that
late point in universal cycles would
be stamping around the designated
planet, then Hir DNA would
joyfully take care of the rest.
A cellular memory, of
sorts, would be passed down
through time to be triggered
at the appropriate point,
alerting Nöé...

Those who have studied the morphology of biological life on the many inhabited planets of the seven superuniverses have commented on the unexpected uniformity of the physical bodies of most intelligent life forms. There were exceptions, of course. Aquatic species might come in many different shapes and sizes, yet on most habitable worlds the indigenous intelligent species were recognizably and surprisingly similar. Sentient life in most cases has appeared to favor a bilateral, symmetrical, humanoid, physical form, regardless of size and evolutionary origin. And perhaps more significantly, this engaging similarity has become progressively more common in the recent eras of the development of the Multiverse.

The wisdom of this arrangement can be observed in the interest and excitement with which a planet's inhabitants will greet the universe broadcast news from other worlds, and in the ease of identifying that all created beings are part of one universal family. It also allowed for a sense of familiarity amongst the various species that attain interstellar travel when they encountered one another in their explorations. The vastness of the Multiverse ensured that these encounters were relatively rare occurrences, which only served to heighten the mutual delight when their paths did eventually cross. As different tribes of aboriginal nomads might move across the continents of their home planet, meeting other nomadic groups in their wanderings and gathering in their *corroborrees*, these interstellar extraterrestrials enjoyed celebrating their encounters with dance and song and the telling of the stories that defined them.

There were a very few amongst the most ancient of these intergalactic travelers who had mastered the high science necessary to manipulate wormholes as a technique for moving rapidly through the spacetime continuum. This had resulted in most of the travel between planets being relatively localized, almost always restricted to those solar systems within the travelers' galaxy of origin.

Space travel has tended to follow much the same arc of development on all technologically advanced worlds. After an initial burst of enthusiasm and some investigations of nearby planets, the inhospitable conditions and the harsh reality of interstellar distances gradually ends up discouraging further exploration. In most cases, a race's ability to move into space is paralleled by an era of rapid spiritual development on its home planet. All planetary cultures, space-faring or not, ultimately evolve from their animal natures to their race's highest spiritual and intellectual potential.

At a certain point in this evolution, when each individual has reached a point of inner realization, the entire planetary culture enters the period of psychic synchronization known as being settled in Light and Life by the *Multiverse Administration (MA)*. As the race shifts to a higher frequency it meets new and different challenges. And so it goes, climbing ever-upward on the grand ladder of Creation, a seemingly endless process of self-perfection, both individual and communal, until the entire living Multiverse becomes one harmonious, dynamic, Whole.

...now securely lodged
within the planet's eco-system,
of the mission
stretching before Hir.

However,
since all the indigenous
species were so different
genotypically from the Helianx,
Noe would have to
use every one of Hir
psychic skills to produce
a reasonable cross-
species symbiosis.

In short, to get laid by the locals.

The common denominator of the planets proposed as being the best choices for Nöé's placement was that they all fell within the lowest habitable frequencies of the Multiverse. The computers had stressed it was only there that Nöé would find biological life sufficiently dense enough to resist the tidal stresses of a spacetime continuum reversal.

The computers had found it well-nigh impossible to unearth data gathered from previous reversals. There was even some doubt as to whether these events had actually occurred before. Some of the younger Helianx, perhaps not entirely trusting the computers' analysis, felt that the whole mission was fruitless. The idea of spending the intervening time, and who knew how long that was going to be, in suspended animation, was not something that appealed to them. Rather, they suggested, all 210 of them should take their chances and throw themselves on the mercy of the natural course of Multiverse evolution. They argued that no one could really predict what the future would bring. And surely, if they could just hold on, they were ingenious enough to discover another way out that was less radical. In the opinion of the Elders, and many of those who had survived their planet's extinction, this had been an outrageous suggestion. They were quick to remind the dissenters that, had their species thrown themselves on the natural course of events on Womb Planet, they would all be long extinct.

After much weighing of consequences, the Helianx had come to peace in their minds and had stabilized the Web sufficiently for what was going to be demanded of them. Nöé, much to all of their surprise, had appeared to take to the concept almost immediately. Granted, sHe had experienced some moments of self-doubt, as the full weight of the responsibilities that lay ahead had sunk in. As with any long-range plan, there was so much that could go wrong. What would happen if Nöé selected the wrong species with which to meld? What if the species sHe chose destroyed itself before it had achieved the ability to move into space? Then, there was always the possibility that the very density of chosen species would work against hir and swamp hir genetic contribution in the volatile tussle of emotions that such a polarized existence had been observed to produce.

The computers did their best to reassure the more nervous Elders that, regardless of the undeniable risks, this plan really did represent their best chance of survival. Their analysis of the potential worlds targeted had predicted that the three potential solar systems chosen were all dense enough to not be unduly influenced by the stresses inherent in a such a reversal. They also reminded the Helianx, with a hint of impatience, of the enormous amount of information stored in their data banks on the various techniques that evolution used to develop sentient life on the planets visited in their galactic wanderings. Although they concurred that no prediction could be made with absolute certainty as to what form a species might ultimately adopt, the planet they had chosen represented the very best chance for the survival of the Helianx.

In short,

to get laid
by the locals.

The intense telepathic bonding that the Helianx had evolved over the millions of years of their history had become the bedrock of their lives. It had allowed them the mental agility to concoct extraordinary advancements in the psychobiological sciences and it had shown them how to make contact with the Heart of Matter. It had formed the center of their social relationships, bringing a transparency that would bewilder a more individuated species; and most importantly, it had led to the creation of the Web. And it was this that, in turn, had given the Helianx access to the immense power available in the arts of focused psychic attention.

The origins of the Web suggests that it had formed originally as a result of their aquatic background and had further expanded when the Helianx had discovered how to travel in the astral realms. The Web had also been invaluable, in conjunction with the computers, with the design and fashioning of the Great Ship. There is also little doubt that, over time, the Helianx grew to rely too much on the organizing principle inherent in the Web when developing their biotechnology. Latter-day galactic historians have speculated that it may well have been this very dependency that had led, idiosyncratically, to the discovery of the *Hub* and the consequent opening to the more occulted powers of the Web.

The Web could best be considered as an ever-shifting, high frequency matrix through which mental telepathic activity can flow. Over time, this dynamic matrix formed in the collective mental body of the Helianx, shaped both by the subtle currents of projected thought acting on higher frequency matter, and the Web's own autonomous responses as a self-organizing principle.

The Hub was a far more imponderable affair. It had remained a mystery to the Helianx through much of their galactic wanderings, only coming to light in momentary, provocative flashes of coherence that had hinted of still deeper mysteries. The Hub can be thought of as the psychic center of the Web, a lens or a focusing device, capable of producing a wide variety of effects.

A direct experience of the Hub quickly became the grail of the inner work practiced by the Helianx on their interminable journeys through interstellar space. They had had enough brief glimpses individually into this harmonious and resonant state to have theorized that something significantly different might occur if a small number of them were to gather in the elaborate, moment-by-moment, psychic balancing act required for a full-blown connection to the Hub. And, by all accounts, occur it did.

After some further experimentation, it became apparent to the Helianx that the level of intimacy required for contact with the Hub was almost entirely dependent on the composition of the individuals participating. While this might not be surprising to a more individuated species, it serves to illustrate one of the challenges facing a telepathic race: An unrealistic grandiosity leading to a spiritual complacency that can manifest as an unfortunate result of the merging of so many powerful minds.

Ai! Yi!! Yi!!!

The music and poetry on that long, last night. Stories, fables, songs, poems, haikus, koans, sonnets, sonatas and even some rock 'n' roll,

...all that the Helianx had ever lifted from the rhymes and rhythms of a million civilizations coalesced, echoing and shimmering along the empathic infraspeak network, which bonded them all into one vast identity.

A gradual introduction to the wealth of information held in the virtual dimensions of the Hub, with its implicit stress on the quality of an individual's consciousness, had been a timely reminder for the Helianx of the value of maintaining a unique personality, while simultaneously being able to lose themselves in the ecstatic closeness of the Web.

Their tentative explorations of the Hub soon revealed that when the Web was coherent and balanced, select groups of individual Helianx were able to meld their collective consciousness with the Hub in a way that made it possible to access the primary dimensions of life in the Multiverse. Although the Helianx had long been aware of the astral realms and had made extensive use of them in their travels out-of-the-body, and their theoretical physicists had always spoken of the multilevel nature of reality, prior to this breakthrough they had no idea how to gain access to these primary dimensions.

The simplicity of this revelation had been shocking at first and yet, as the physicists amongst them were quick to point out, the answer had been staring them in the face ever since their forebears had first proposed that the universe might have a multilayered structure. It had been then that the Helianx had started calling it the Multiverse. It was only by including the existence of enfolded dimensions that they were able to explain to themselves the aid they had often received so mysteriously in times of crisis. Just as planet-bound astronomers might infer the presence of a world invisible to their telescopes by measuring the small perturbations of its parent star, so also had the Helianx deduced the reality of these other dimensions by carefully observing the nature of the synchronous events that had been increasingly occurring in their lives. As a consequence, they had grown to believe that other sentient life existed on these finer dimensions, life that had appeared to have the best interests of their species at heart. But, try as they might, the Helianx had never been able to directly interact in any way with these caring beings.

As the millennia passed, a growing number of Helianx gained a working familiarity with the subtle energies of the Hub. This had encouraged them to make far more accurate maps of these exotic new dimensions, so unlike anywhere else they had visited in their previous explorations. Great *Architectural Worlds* were charted, far larger than anything even the Helianx had encountered, majestically orbiting stars in the fifth dimension and supporting countless myriad of celestial creatures. At other times, *Energy Beings* might flash across their field of vision, busy about their unknowable functions, unheeding and implacable. And yet, at another moment, some of the more experimental amongst them would find themselves deposited deep in the uninhabited outer limits of the Multiverse, dancing in the first dimension to the long, slow, rhythms of the rock devas, as they molded the forms of the worlds to come.

It had taken aeons of devoted practice and many generations for the Helianx to learn how to navigate collaboratively in these strange new dimensions, so oddly different from the universes of time and space they had come to know in their travels through the primary dimensions of the Multiverse.

The anticipation and the wonderment of this ancient race of space gypsies all joined into a single concentrated stream of focussed energy, and entered into the prana of their chosen representative, a diplomat, if you like...

By the time the computers had announced their audacious plan for the survival of the Helianx, the space gypsies had mastered enough of the subtleties of the Hub to be able to move with relative ease through the primary dimensions. Regardless, it had been a humbling learning experience for them. Having become accustomed to thinking of themselves as the oldest and wisest race they had ever encountered in their travels, it had shaken them deeply to observe the true hidden workings of the Multiverse. As an inherently indolent species, accustomed to taking their physical reality somewhat for granted, they found themselves strangely shamed by their glimpses of what was going on behind the scrim of reality.

At the higher frequencies, magnificent beings, entities, forces and energies, some personified and some not, but all well beyond the current comprehension of the Helianx, fulfilled their wide-ranging celestial functions in the Multiverse Administration. The Helianx had felt slightly more comfortable In the lower, more ponderous, frequencies of the worlds in-the-making; those of the rock, floral and animal dimensions, despite the inherent violence they observed on those levels. The Helianx had become aware of the intelligence inherent in the natural world prior to the revelations of the Hub, yet they had to admit to themselves that until then they had no idea of the extraordinary complexity of devic life which lay behind the organization of physical matter.

Planetary anthropologists have since speculated that it was their very bio-technological skills that had blind-sided the Helianx to the true nature of these devic dimensions. They had never had a need-to-know. The catastrophe that had propelled them off Womb Planet, and their subsequent collective emotional trauma, had also fed a growing skepticism as to whether the Multiverse really was as benign as their legendary songs had insisted.

As the Helianx became more adept at melding with the Hub, their doubts had dropped away when they started to appreciate the difficulties faced by virtually every level of sentient life. On the very highest rungs of the ladder of functional intelligence the Helianx had watched those magnificent celestials in the sixth and seventh dimensions, working with an almost mechanical diligence to lay down the spiritual circuitry upon which the smooth administration of the Multiverse depended. But, as the Helianx became more familiar with the lower three dimensions, they were initially astonished to realize the challenges that had helped to shape life into its most basic forms, grew more violent as they descended the dimensional ladder. At the most fundamental level of planetary organization stars blasted out white-hot plasma; worlds heaved with volcanism; asteroids smashed heedlessly onto the already-pitted surfaces of planets and moons; oceans carved into cliffs, and torrential rivers and glaciers sliced their way through mountains. When organic life eventually emerged on a planet, it seemed to the Helianx that the evolutionary processes employed were no less brutal. Up and down the food chain predators preyed on other creatures; massive die-offs and extinctions invariably followed as different species fought for survival and dominance.

It was not a pretty picture, but it was one that their computers had insisted that Nöé would need to experience if sHe was to complete hir mission.

The anticipation and
the wonderment of
this ancient race
of space gypsies
all joined into a
single, concentrated,
stream of focussed
energy and entered into
the prâna of their
chosen
representative,
a diplomat, if
you like...

spun off out
into the great vortex
of the space/time
continuum.

encoded,
hopefully,
with the key
which will
in due time lead
Noë to release Hir
loved ones
from cold
storage.

All fears and doubts had to be put aside when the Helianx assembled to meld with the Hub for the most important gathering of their lives. The Elders noted that Nöé seemed to be the least concerned with the dangers sHe was bound to have to face on the planet of choice. Whether this was a sign of Nöé's naiveté, a product of hir long sojourns in the harsh conditions of the desert simulacrum, or simply a confirmation of the rightness of the computers' unpredictable selection, the Elders were not able to discern. Although they sincerely hoped that it was the latter.

It took longer than usual for the assembled Helianx to harmonize their psychic integrity with the Web. The excitement that many of them felt as they started to come together had to be released into the Web before they could access the Hub. The intensity of these emotions required a constant psychic balancing act, as each tried to do their part in bringing the Web into equilibrium. This was not something their otherwise invaluable computers could help them with, but demanded all the psycho-spiritual resources that the Helianx had been able to garner in their philosophical reveries.

The necessity of perfectly harmonizing the Web prior to probing deeper had always been the most difficult part of working with the Hub. It seemed to the Helianx that this was the way the Hub protected its secrets from possible abuse. Apparently only those who were capable of an advanced state of relaxed concentration, and a meditative quietness of mind and heart, were open to being upstepped into the mysterious wonders of the Hub. Paradoxically, it was only when the collective Spirit of the Helianx had moved into the Hub's powerful vortex, that the intensity of emotional focus built up sufficiently to allow them fluid transport through the dimensions.

It was this radical shift of consciousness, from the meditative equilibrium of the Web to the directed passion of the Hub, that had proved so consistently difficult for the Helianx to master. From the time that the first small group had stumbled on the Hub, it had taken many generations for all 210 to gain a reasonable facility at making this transition. Predictably enough, this had been made all the more challenging since what they were about to do-- to send one of their number sliding down through the spacetime continuum--had never previously been attempted.

In order to achieve a lens of sufficient clarity to create a localized wormhole, each individual Helianx had to navigate this difficult passage before starting the songs that had been recommended to activate the appropriate warp in space. The computers had assured them that it was this precise sequence of tonal frequencies, together with the passion with which the songs were delivered, that was guaranteed to trigger the inner coherence of the Hub. From that point on, the Hub would essentially take over and focus the lens in such a way that it would allow Nöé to move easily from the security of the Great Ship and the companionship of hir kind, to an unpredictable destiny, alone and isolated, on a distant planet.

...spun off out
into the great vortex
of the space/time
continuum,

encoded,
hopefully,
with the key
which will
in due time lead
Nöe to release Hir
loved ones
from cold
storage.

Life on Earth, on the planet was
known colloquially after the substance
covering everything, not well...
Ah! well
Well, life on Earth was not a
straightforward affair.

It was only very exceptional circumstances that brought all 210 Helianx physically together in the vast central chamber of the Great Ship. Their telepathic abilities, although limited in reach to a distance of about half-a-million miles, allowed them to spend almost all their time placidly basking in their individual baths of nutrient jelly, connected to each other only by the constantly fascinating dynamics of was happening on the Web.

The central chamber, filled with sea water of the same chemical composition as the ocean of Womb Planet, formed the nexus of the maze of interconnecting canals which led, in turn, to the nutrient domes, and then on down through a series of water-locks to the terra-formed simulacra in the nether regions of the craft.

The organic structure of the Great Ship, fashioned from the same basic bioplasm as the Helianx and treated to absorb and dissipate harmful solar radiation, allowed for a high degree of flexibility. The massive chambers, the communication pods, the many nutrient domes, the planetary museums and simulacra, the spider's web of canals, and all the ancillary areas needed for the cosmic gypsy life, would have appeared to an observer every bit like the internal organs of an immense creature.

The containing walls of the ship could peristaltically expand and contract, gently moving the water to where it was needed, opening and closing valves as required. The temperature and salinity, as well as the precise balance of supplements in the nutrient domes, were all controlled autonomously by the craft's cybernetic intelligence. Because this semi-sentient system had long been linked to the telepathic Web, it permitted the ship to sense in realtime whatever it was that the Helianx needed. Vision screens, apparently unbidden, might ripple down before them when they needed to examine an intriguing planet; bulkheads and dry platforms emerged spontaneously on the rare occasions the Elders had teleported land-based ambassadors aboard; the great wings, stretching endlessly into the galactic night, responded from moment to moment to the vagaries of the cosmic winds; and what the craft could not handle on its own in the tedium of intergalactic space, their prescient computers had well in hand.

Some contemporary exopsychologists have suggested that the act of handing over so much power to their technology, however sentient it might be, greatly contributed to the progressive weakening of the life-force of the Helianx race. Other academics have even speculated that given normal circumstances, the entire species might have died out from terminal ennui well before the anticipated gravitational stresses ever threatened to tear apart their bodies.

On the day of the gathering, however, the Helianx had known that they would have to summon all their inner resources to sing the correct sequence of tones to activate the wormhole. They all understood that it was their last, and if the computers were to be believed, their only chance of survival. It had been this harsh reality, not surprisingly, that had jolted even the most passive Helianx into doing hir passionate best.

Life on Earth, as the planet was known colloquially after the substance covering everything not wet... Ah! wet! Well, life on Earth was not a straightforward affair.

Unlike Womb Planet, there seemed to be an almost endless profusion of life-forms... all struggling against apparently ridiculous odds for survival ...and their own ecological niches.

Having arranged themselves in the three concentric circles that they used on the rare occasions they gathered for collective ritual, the Elders placed Nöé in the center of the innermost circle. The young Helianx had been extensively briefed on what was required of hir. While the remaining 209 of hir race balanced and harmonized the Web prior to giving themselves collectively over to the ecstasy of the Hub, Nöé was required to focus hir entire energy on what they all had traditionally most disdained, that of maintaining the integrity of hir individual consciousness. To any telepathic species, the joy and stimulation of a group mind was a powerful and addictive draw and the Helianx were no exception. Any idea of breaking completely free of the Web had become anathema to them. It had been this taboo that originally so concerned the Elders, when they had observed Nöé's proclivity for hir lengthy visits to the desert simulacrum.

As the Web was brought into equilibrium and the songs of the Helianx gained in passion and momentum, the psychic potency of the Hub started blossoming open, forming a glowing sheath of ultimatonic energy that revolved around Nöé at an ever-increasing speed. These particular moments, according to the computer analysis, were the most crucial, as the emerging wormhole had to be held open and stable long enough for Nöé to make the transition to hir new destination.

Wormhole manipulation and the art of folding the spacetime continuum was a relatively recent discovery and had emerged naturally, as the Helianx gained confidence in working with the Hub. During their long, last tour of the early superuniverses, the Hub, apparently responding to necessity and the pressure of time, had introduced them to the technique of co-creating sufficiently dynamic wormholes to move the Great Ship light-years across intergalactic space in a single moment. But it was one thing to transport the craft, and themselves, to the other end of the same superuniverse and quite another to focus specifically on a single individual and consign them to another superuniverse entirely. This was to be the first and last time, hopefully, that such a ritual would have to be used. Realizing this deepened the trance and helped empower the Helianx to maintain the needed momentum and purity of tone.

For Nöé, at the center of all this psychophysical activity, hir struggle to retain an individuated consciousness, while the rest of hir race melded with the Hub, was perhaps the most difficult state of mind sHe had ever attempted. SHe knew from the ship's previous hyper-spacial jumps that the transition was extremely rapid. At one moment sHe would be on the Ship and the next sHe would find hirself deposited on the surface of a strange new world. Nurturing this thought and willing hirself to relax became the key to holding onto hir individuated consciousness, while the surrounding vortex spun faster and faster.

Nöé closed hir many eyes to shut out the dizzying spectacle, and drawing deeply into hirself sHe turned hirself over to ministrations of the Hub. Whatever was to happen next would seal hir fate and ultimately that of hir entire species.

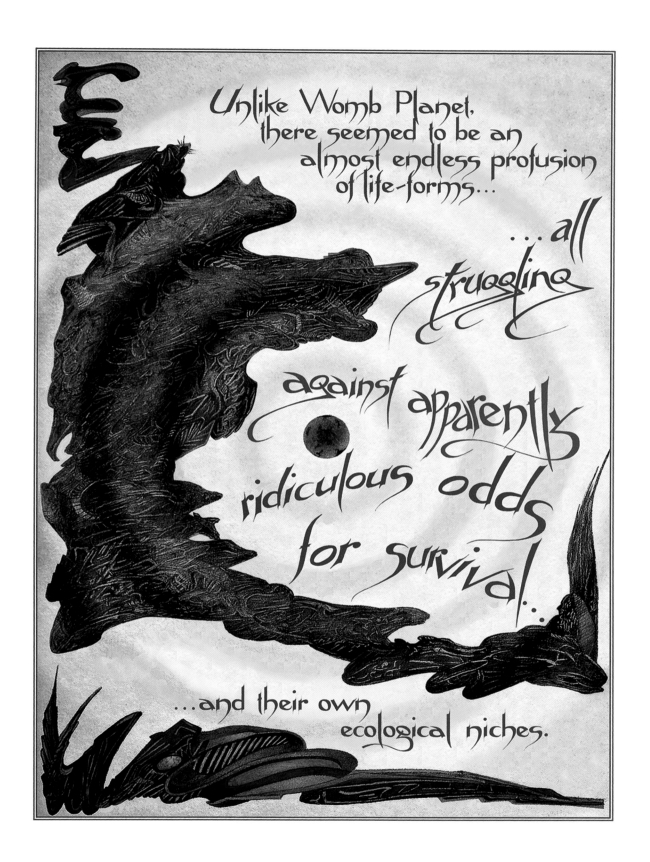

Unlike Womb Planet, there seemed to be an almost endless profusion of life-forms...

...all struggling against apparently ridiculous odds for survival...

...and their own ecological niches.

When Nöé returned to full consciousness and opened hir eyes sHe found hirself alone and sprawled across a flat, sandy plain, very similar to the desert sHe had so often visited in the hold of the Great Ship. Whether this placement was purely fortuitous, or more likely, that it had been programmed into the Hub as the optimal destination of the localized wormhole, Nöé could only guess. But, sHe was grateful for the unexpected familiarity. SHe was unable to retain any memory of hir transit through the spacetime continuum except for an overpowering inner sense of the color blue. Even now, as sHe gazed around at hir arid new surroundings, sHe could still see a vague sheen of ethereal blue shimmering around the edges of the distant mountains.

As the computers had assured hir, Nöé was able to absorb the surface atmosphere through her skin. Although the composition of the air was slightly different from what sHe had been told, it appeared to be perfectly viable for short periods out of the water. Not having air-breathing lungs in the manner of the many indigenous creatures sHe was later to encounter, Nöé was grateful for all the times sHe had been able to spend in the simulated desert, getting accustomed to life out of the water. She soon noticed a definite shift in hir consciousness. Whether this was caused by diminished oxygenation, or more likely, by hir delight in the considerably lessened gravitational field of the planet, sHe did not want to consider until sHe had fully recovered from the transit.

Nöé's thoughts turned back to hir life on the ship and how sHe had been shunned by so many of hir companions for flouting the strictly-held taboo surrounding hir activities in the simulacra. Even though sHe always made sure to close down hir access to the Web before sHe set out for the desert, news of hir short flights had leaked out and it had become increasingly difficult to disguise the growth of the small wings along the length of hir body. With the exception of a few of the more enlightened Elders, who had silently encouraged Nöé to trust the wisdom of hir heart, most of the Helianx had been horrified. Nightmarish memories of the crushing forces they had encountered back on Womb Planet flooded through the Web, throwing the younger ones into a panicked overreaction. That had not endeared Nöé to the others.

Alone on a strange world and out of contact with the Web, Nöé was able to more fully appreciate how elegantly sHe had been trained for this mission. After growing accustomed to the strong gravitational field in the simulated desert, sHe could now revel in this new lightness of being. At last sHe could flex hir small wings without fear of censure; the rays of the single sun glinting off iridescent scales as spasms of pure pleasure rippled down hir massive body. A soft wind blew in from what Nöé's sensitive skin told hir was a nearby ocean, the slight salinity in the air stimulating rather more pleasant memories of life on the Great Ship.

The warming rays of the sun; the scented air; the resilience of the sand under hir soft, white body; and a perfectly natural exhaustion; all this came together to draw Nöé into a deeply introspective and meditative state.

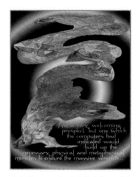

Many passages of sun and moon had passed before Nöé awoke from hir long meditation, alert and suddenly aware of odd, and somewhat painful, sensations that seemed to emanate from where one of hir segmented flanks lay across a small fertile valley. Turning hir body to find out what was causing the pain, sHe was able to see small creatures clinging to hir sides, their teeth buried in hir soft flesh. Others, thrown off by hir movement, were lumbering away in terror for the safety of the trees, their heavily-armored bodies lurching and colliding with one another in their haste.

Although Nöé had been briefed by the computers on the results of the Uniscan and thus had a broad knowledge of the life forms on this third planet from the sun, sHe was unprepared and surprised at the immediate hostility that hir presence provoked. There was never any threat, of course, since hir enormous size prevented any real damage to hir body. But emerging, as sHe had, from a gentle and non-aggressive background, sHe found this unrestrained animosity both annoying and downright discourteous.

In their journeys through the inhabited universes, the Helianx had uniscanned many worlds on which primitive life was developing, but had never directly interacted with any of the wide variety of simple creatures observed. There had never been a good reason, since the clues for which the Helianx were searching were only to be found on planets on which life had evolved to a point at which it could ponder its own nature and its place in the universe. When this milestone had been achieved, it was the function of administrating agents sent out from MA to activate the relevant universe broadcast circuits, allowing the inhabitants a far deeper and more detailed understanding of the way the Multiverse worked.

While the computers were making their final choices as to which world would give Nöé the best chance of survival, the fourth planet within the same solar system was presented as a distinct possibility. Some of the Elders had favored this choice in spite of its small size and its generally cool overall temperature. The oceans were deep and water was plentiful and the inhabitants were well on their way to evolving a high level of intelligence. However, when the computers ran their predictive programs, it quickly became apparent that deteriorating planetary conditions would be likely to force the inhabitants off their world well before the designated time.

Patiently, the computers had explained that timing was the single most important factor in the entire enterprise. Although the fourth planet possessed many of the necessary requirements, intelligent life was predicted to be too far advanced for Nöé's purposes. Besides, sHe would need many more millions of years than would have been available to hir to adjust to a reasonable size to complete hir replicatory function. This metamorphic process would dictate both the appropriate timing for Nöé's primary mission, as well as hir eventual symbiotic reemergence within the inner biological lives of what would become the dominant host species.

Not a very welcoming
prospect, but one which
the computers had
indicated would
build up the
necessary physical and metaphysical
muscles to endure the massive wrench...

It had not been easy for the Helianx to accept their computers' assessment of what was to become of the Multiverse. To many of the Elders it had seemed counterintuitive for Whoever--or Whatever-- had created them in the first place, to then deposit them for a second time no less, into an almost impossible situation. Surely their long lives and all the knowledge they had accumulated had to count for something. To think that it would all be destroyed along with their beloved descendants, who, because of their race's practice of serial reincarnation, would also be them, was too horrifying by far to even consider.

It had only been the patient reassurances of their omniscient computers that had persuaded them that they would all find a way through this impending disaster with enough effort and time, and it had been this confidence that had encouraged the Helianx, after much dithering, to adopt their desperate plan. Nöé understood the planet that would be hir home, for who knew how long, had been chosen primarily because it was in a solar system close to the rim of a galactic spiral within the seventh superuniverse. This choice would hopefully ensure that sHe had enough time to adapt successfully to hir new life in whatever physical form sHe would finally find hirself, allowing hir ultimately to release hir loved ones from suspended animation.

For Nöé, however, these thoughts were fading fast as sHe struggled to maintain hir equilibrium in the light of the many new sensations currently assailing hir. For all its superficial similarities to the desert simulacrum sHe had known so well on the Great Ship, the planet on which sHe found hirself was very different. Breezes that never blew over the desert wastes in the ship now caressed hir sensitive skin; the distant mountains implied a scale far beyond anything possible in the hold of the Great Ship; the taste of the air was quite unlike anything Nöé had previously experienced, thick and pungent with chlorophyl; the rhythms of night and day, which had never been duplicated in the simulations, introduced an unanticipated pulse into hir new life. There was so much for which the computers had been unable to prepare hir.

The sun warmed Nöé's somnolent body. SHe could feel the Earth under hir, alive and welcoming. Trees tickled hir flanks. As the days followed nights, sHe noticed the creatures that initially attacked hir, were now thankfully no longer interested in lunging at hir flesh. SHe could only assume that hir alien biology was unpalatable to the local fauna, as sHe could not help but notice, with a shudder that rippled down hir entire body, that the beasts continued to voraciously devour one another. Strange flying creatures dived and circled around Nöé's enormous head, but after some awkward attempts to alight on hir silky skin, they also lost interest and flapped away toward the mountains.

Nöé rested. The physical and metaphysical shock of transiting a wormhole intact gradually diminished while sHe dreamed of hir life on the Great Ship and the tender closeness of hir companions; of the warmth and brilliance of the Web; of the endless panorama of interstellar space; and of their songs of discovery and the scintillating depths of their accumulated knowledge.

However, regardless of the provocations of the native life-forms,

the one-gravity of Earth proved to be a splendid stomping ground for Nöé — the lone Helianx.

Since the Helianx were such a long-lived race, time passed in a very different way from how it was experienced by most other species. The Space Gypsies had first encountered this profound disparity in many of the races they had tried to warn of the impending universe reversal. It seemed that for these races time was governed by the rotational rhythms of their home planets, or amongst the more advanced species, by the measured vibration of atoms. The Helianx considered this to be sequential time, and although they recognized attempts to standardize time as having value in plotting galactic navigation, they had never lost their innate ability to vividly experience a more subjective time.

Sequential time, as they all knew, was an inescapable aspect of the spacetime continuum, and due to localized gravitational forces was subject to a limited expansion and compression. These anomalies were well understood by most intelligent space-faring species, so regardless of the problems, there emerged a common language to discuss the nature of time and reality.

Subjective time, for the Helianx, was something quite different. By controlling the quality of their meditational trances, they were able to manipulate their inner experience of the passage of time, speeding it up or slowing it down at will. This ability, present to a limited extent in most sentient creatures, had been brought to a fine art by the Helianx, and had allowed them to cover the vast intergalactic distances without being driven insane by the tedium of space. Of course, while the Helianx were in their trance, sequential time would be ticking away; planets were circling their stars in their predictably regular orbits, and caesium-133 atoms continued to oscillate in their atomic clocks. There was no avoiding the inevitability of sequential time, but at least the Helianx had learned how to avoid becoming enslaved by it.

So it was for Nöé, alone on a strange new world. SHe was half-aware of the regular pulsing of night and day; of a single moon speeding across a star-studded sky; of the changing of the seasons and the occasional shaking of the earth on which sHe lay. Yet little disturbed hir dreams while hir enormous body made its own autonomous adjustments to its new environment.

When Nöé finally felt sHe had recuperated sufficiently to make hir first moves in this strange new landscape, sHe realized that sHe had no idea of how long sHe had been resting motionless. SHe tentatively unfurled hir small wings, three rows of them arranged along hir full length, which glinted with a coppery glow in the evening sunlight. Then, as sHe shrugged off the debris that had accumulated over hir while she had lain there, sHe flapped hir wings with a little more vigor, sending an undulating wave of movement down hir long body. To hir astonishment, sHe started gradually to lift off from where sHe was lying, hovering with almost no effort about 50 feet above the ground. SHe recalled, without much pleasure, how much sHe had struggled to coordinate hir newly bestowed wings back at the simulacrum, let alone to get off the ground.

Life on this world, Nöé realized with a newfound and growing confidence, was going to be very different from anything sHe could have anticipated.

However,
regardless of the provocations
of the native life-forms,

the one-gravity of Earth
proved to be a splendid
stamping ground
for Nöé,
the lone
Helianx.

Hir feathery wings, though diminutive, were perfectly suitable for short flights.

Nöé soon found that SHe was able to mix a little more indistinguishably with the planet's then-dominant species, a reptilian rabble of dubious and extremely limited intelligence.

Although Nöé had been briefed on what sHe might expect from the electromagnetic and gravitational forces present on the planet, the vastly lessened pressure of gravity only added to hir growing feeling of comfort, even of pleasure. Not quite the sense of weightlessness sHe remembered from hir previous lives floating in the oceans of Womb Planet, but a buoyancy-of-being that filled hir with a profound joy.

In light of this, Nöé's sorrow at being separated from hir loved ones gradually dissipated, as hir short flights grew more far-flung and adventurous. There was so much to explore and Nöé, as all Helianx, was an extremely curious creature. SHe knew from the Uniscan analysis that at this point in the evolution of planetary life there were no animals of an appreciable intelligence present on this world. But that was of lesser importance to Nöé than the extraordinary profusion of different life forms that seemed to mutate while sHe watched. Hir great size and hir ability to remain motionless for long periods of time--a necessary talent for the intergalactic traveler--rendered hir all but invisible to most indigenous life. This allowed hir to observe the frenetic activity that surrounded hir, whenever sHe settled hir body down onto the welcoming earth.

The changing of the seasons; the pounding of rivers swollen with melting snow; streams of lava pouring down the side of a volcano; waterfalls that towered over even Nöé's vast bulk; the constantly changing jungles, grasslands and deserts; the many songs of the earth that curled up to hir sensitive receptors; all this and more was so novel and fascinating that sHe had completely forgotten the first tempting scent of the sea. SHe had become so entranced by all the new sensations that overcame hir, as sHe took hir short flights around the continent on which sHe found hirself, that sHe was astonished when sHe once again picked up the sweet smell of the ocean.

Perhaps it was a sense of delayed gratification that held her back, hir towering bulk lining the seashore like a range of hills and the salt-laden winds stroking the length of hir sensitive body. SHe knew from the computers' predictions that the oceans of this world would have to be hir home for many millions of years to come, and that there would be signs made obvious to hir as to when sHe would need to leave the water for the land. Nöé would later justify hir long delay by thinking back nostalgically to the songs of the Earth and how both their spirits had danced together in their shared dreams.

The celestial beings, whose function it was to nurture the planet through the millions of years that evolution took to produce intelligent life, had been initially surprised at Nöé's arrival. They had not been briefed on how to respond to such an unexpected event. Their subsequent attempts to get more information out of MA's local administration had only resulted in a vague reassurance that Nöé's appearance must have been sanctioned at the very highest levels of MA's bureaucracy, because they had been told nothing of it.

Hir leathery wings,
though diminutive,
were perfectly suitable for short flights.

Nöé soon found that SHe was able
to mix a little more
indistinguishably
with the planet's then-dominant species,
a reptilian rabble of dubious
and extremely limited intelligence.

Nöé slowly became aware of the changes that had been taking place within hir body, autonomously adjusting hir to the slightly different conditions of planetary life. Unfamiliar bacteria were analyzed and assimilated, as hir sensitive internal organs reconfigured themselves to cope with the denser vibrational structure of matter. Over time, sHe found the substance of hir body drawing in and compacting, hir great size gradually diminishing as the millennia passed. Within 40 million years sHe found that hir size had been reduced from a little over three miles long to a mere mile and a quarter.

Long ago all Helianx had learned the advantages of delegating many of their internal biological processes to their *Indwelling Devas*. It had freed their minds to focus on what had always interested them most, their endless journey of discovery into the vastness of the mental and spiritual realms that had so enriched their long lives. They had come to think of their bodies merely as vehicles, as houses, that they had turned over to caretakers to care for while they were traveling out of them. This had resulted in a level of devic autonomy which had allowed the Helianx to adjust to a wide variety of physical conditions, and was largely responsible for their reputation as intergalactic shapeshifters.

Nöé, however, had been advised by the computers that sHe would need to establish a far more collaborative relationship with hir deva, if sHe was to modify hir body sufficiently to accomplish the mission. SHe had not originally greeted this information from the computers with much enthusiasm. It had felt like a backward step to hir, since it was a matter of some pride that the Helianx had managed to detach themselves so completely from their bodies.

Once on the planet, and as sHe came to terms with her future prospects, Nöé quickly recognized the wisdom of the computers' counsel. Hir prime intention for the foreseeable future would have to focus on preparing hirself, on keeping hirself safe through many millions of years of climatic changes and the inevitable planetary disasters. SHe needed to hone hir body and spirit for the time sHe would be able to pass on the Helianx DNA to the appropriate host species. And the only way this was going to be accomplished was to work very closely with hir deva.

These were the thoughts that were running through hir somnolent mind, as Nöé lay along the coastline, lazily prolonging the moment sHe knew sHe had to move hir life into the sea. Hir explorations on land had already been rich enough and hir natural curiosity had allowed sufficient time for hir body to adapt to the many viral and bacteriological challenges this new world presented.

However profuse the flora and fauna were on land, it turned out to be nothing compared to what Nöé observed when sHe did finally enter the ocean. Swimming creatures of every shape and size circled around hir massive head, as sHe sunk deeper into the cool water. Seaweed as tall as forest trees stroked hir belly and small fish burrowed into the sandy seabed when hir shadow passed over them. Life seemed to be everywhere sHe looked, as sHe swam slowly with the tide, hugging the coastline and relishing the velvet sweep of water over the length of hir body.

After some brief and somewhat unsuccessful attempts at parthenogenesis, Nöe plumped for an internal modification of Hir own genetics, a technique known to all Helianx.

SHe blocked Hir histones, stripped back Hir RNA, expressed this, supressed that, and sent long, complex messages to Hir DNA codes.

...in a wild, convoluted dance
with Hir own chromosomes.

until
finally, Nöe arrived at
something
approaching
a convenient
size
for the
planet.

After some more millions of years,
sHe even contracted a throat virus,
dropped on the place...

The Helianx had always known that whichever world was chosen for Nöé's long exile, hir enormous size was inevitably going to be one of the most important issues with which sHe would have to deal. In their extensive travels they had never encountered any other intelligent species quite as large as themselves. This had even become something of an embarrassment on the rare occasions when diplomats of other planetary cultures had insisted on being teleported up to the Great Ship. The awe that these huge creatures would habitually inspire in their diminutive guests did little to encourage intelligent discussion, and frequently had resulted in the Helianx being worshipped as divine.

Indeed, had there been another intelligent race roaming the surface of the planet in those early millennia of Nöé's arrival, they too, might well have attributed hir physical changes to godlike powers. But Nöé understood that this was far too early in the evolution of life on this world to expect much beyond animal instincts and the inevitable horror of predation. SHe also knew from hir previous experience that other beings, on subtler frequencies than sHe could perceive, were likely to be more than aware of hir, although sHe could only guess at what they made of hir unexpected appearance.

The celestials, however, having laid down the original patterns of life, now appeared to have stepped back from the evolutionary process, merely to observe the fruits of their labors from the wings. After they had recovered from their initial surprise at Nöé's arrival, and had seen that sHe represented no obvious threat to their plans, they chose simply to ignore hir and trust that MA had its own unknowable reasons for allowing this to occur. They all appreciated that this was an *experimental planet* and apart from the initial modifications they had been encouraged to make in life-design, who really knew what possibilities would unfold as a consequence of Nöé's presence? After watching Nöé's harmless activities for a few more million years, the celestials became reconciled to hir presence. Much to their relief sHe appeared to be almost entirely involved with hir own internal processes and when sHe was not exploring the oceans of hir new world, sHe could be found lying motionless in a state of self-induced hibernation in the cool waters of the southern polar regions.

The only real change the celestials had noticed over the aeons was Nöé's gradual, but persistent, shrinking in size and they agreed between themselves that this was ultimately of no concern to them. MA's instructions, followed faithfully by the celestials since the first planets were seeded with life, were strictly hands-off. Even though the *Life Carriers* were permitted to experiment in the initial stages of evolution, as held true on every tenth planet, once the life processes had taken hold, they were required to step back. The pleasure the celestials then derived from their work lay largely in observing the unanticipated and fascinating interactions between the increasingly complex life forms. Thus it was that Nöé's presence on the planet, over the millions of years, gradually slipped from the collective memory of the celestials. Somewhat later the files mentioning hir few authenticated appearances disappeared in a faulty software upgrade at one of MA's subsidiary reference centers. All that remained were the subtle perturbations in the planet's psychosphere, unnoticed by the emerging life-forms.

...in a wild, convoluted dance
with Hir own chromosomes,

until
finally,

Nöé arrived at
something
approaching
a convenient
size
for the
planet.

After some more millions of years
SHe even contracted a throat virus
dropped on the place...

As the millions of years passed Nöé's presence on the planet was gradually taken for granted. SHe had no reason to interfere with what sHe understood as the normal progress of evolution, since sHe was more than aware that hir mission depended on how well sHe prepared hirself for the times ahead.

Nöé's original decision to employ hir *parthenogenetic* ability to reproduce had served hir well over hir first 40 million years on Earth. As sHe had been advised back on the ship, sHe was careful to restrict the number of eggs that sHe nurtured in hir body at any one time, to three. These three female offspring carried the full Helianx genetic endowment, but as they aged, they also needed to absorb all that Nöé had learned in the course of hir long life. The closeness of the small clan's telepathic bonding assured each of them that when Nöé was preparing to leave hir body for the final time, hir immediate offspring would be ready in their turn to procreate. Then, following the age-old principles of serial reincarnation, Nöé's spirit would settle comfortably over the strongest and most developed of hir progeny, until sHe was ready to start the whole process over again. Over the millions of years, Nöé's many offspring lived and died in the oceans of the world, their enormous bodies decaying and mixing with the calcified remains of all the other indigenous sea creatures.

Parthenogenesis had been a strategy in their reproductive arsenal that the Helianx had used immediately after they had left their devastated world, as a way of building up their numbers as rapidly as possible. Once they had stabilized their small population and had decided to set off on their interstellar adventures, they reverted to more normal sexual reproduction in order to broaden the base of their individual genotypes. Since all Helianx were hermaphrodites, having simultaneously both male and female internal reproductive organs, they were capable of self-fertilization under extreme circumstances. This was the technique that had served Nöé well in the early years of hir exile. Their preference, however, as with most other intelligent species, was a paired mating. Each individual Helianx then consciously chose the male or the female role, deciding between them which genetic combination would be most favorable.

Because the Helianx had traditionally decided to keep their numbers to a stable 210--although none of them could have accounted for quite why this number had been originally chosen--their reproductive imperative, of necessity, was far less pressing than for most species. The telepathic closeness the Helianx experienced through the Web satisfied much of the need for intimacy that other races achieved through family bonding. Their practice of serial reincarnation ensured individual temporal continuity and their sensitive skins had always favored them with the extreme sensual pleasure of physical contact. Over time, these factors were accepted by the Helianx as a happy substitute for the frantic couplings they had observed in more sexually driven species.

Back on the planet Nöé was starting to feel a profound change in the air. The brief visits of other space-faring races, rare at the best of times, had appeared to cease, but not before the last of them had passed on to Nöé some very disturbing information.

...sometime earlier in a panspermic raid by another race of culture vultures.

But, at least now Nöé could speak without knocking the locals back on their asses.

As Nöé decreased her size to a manageable proportion, sHe found hirself forced to become more aware of the other creatures on the planet. If the seas had been filled with hungry snapping maws of every shape and size, Nöé's brief forays onto the land had amazed hir, when sHe found vastly increased populations of dinosaurs filling, and then rapidly destroying, every available ecological niche to which they could adapt.

The planet had apparently exploded with life while Nöé's attention had been consumed with hir tiny clan's survival and hir own demanding biological processes. By this time, hir vastly diminished size presented a more tempting target for the largest of the predatory dinosaurs and this had sent hir scurrying back to the relative safety of the oceans and the reassurance of hir kin.

Nöé was to wonder later at the fortuitous timing of the asteroid that so profoundly changed the development of life on Earth. Although the warning sHe had received from the extraterrestrial visitors had been based on observation, their calculations had not been accurate enough to predict exactly where on the planet the rock would strike. It seemed something of a happy coincidence to Nöé, therefore, when sHe found hirself deep in the ocean and on the other side of the planet that day the asteroid smashed into the coastline of one of the northern continents.

The juddering impact of the asteroid made the Earth ring like a gigantic gong. The sound waves rippled through the oceans, reverberating for days after the event, as the delicious, deep harmonics intertwined and resonated in the buoyancy chambers of Nöé's body. Tidal waves swept overhead; the skies darkened; hurricane-force winds roared around hir head when sHe briefly surfaced. Soon the air was filled with dust particles and had Nöé thought to spend any more time on the surface, sHe would have had to search the sky for the dim glow of a deep red sun, now almost entirely cloaked by an atmosphere thick with smoke and grime.

The scent of the ocean turned to death as the decaying carcasses of large land animals, suffocated by the dirt-filled air and swept into rivers flooded by torrential rains, were ripped to pieces by sharks driven to a frenzy by their unexpected windfall. Tectonic plates heaved and ground against each other, with magma pouring up through newly-opened crevasses and spewing sulfurous gases into the surrounding ocean. Microorganisms like *foraminifera*, and almost all the vegetal matter dependent on photosynthesis, shriveled and died. The small creatures that fed on this dense underwater vegetation quickly followed.

In the deeper waters of the open ocean, life was far less seriously disturbed by the massive shock of the impact. Nöé was relieved, but not surprised, to find the cosmic rays that had faithfully infused hir with energy for so long were not absorbed or deflected by the haze, but continued to pour down from the galactic center. Nöé was safe for the moment.

Time passed.

Nöe's empathic contact was just fine with most species.

SHe routinely sang, and talked to the rocks, and the sea, and the plants.

The undifferentiated consciousness of the planetary life forms was similar to the bonding Nöe had known with Hir own race.

However, by now a new phenomenon had appeared.

When Nöé finally felt it was safe enough to venture back out onto dry land the dust had settled and the skies were clear. What sHe remembered of the landscape had radically changed. Earthquakes generated by the intense impact of the asteroid had rearranged coastlines and she saw mountains that had been wrenched apart by rifts in the earth below. Rivers cascaded down through valleys where previously there had just been a desert plateau. Firestorms had ripped across the globe, incinerating almost all the old growth trees, leaving only a tangled mass of new vegetation struggling for its place in the sun. Massive tidal waves had swept over low-lying islands, extinguishing all remaining life and littering the oceans with the decomposing detritus of a previous era.

A pervasive silence lay over the thick, new jungle and where before the constant roars and cries of predators and victims had filled the air, now Nöé could hear only the faint squeaks and warbles of the smallest of creatures. All of the large reptiles had disappeared, as had most species of small mammals and the reptiles that lived off a diet of stolen dinosaur eggs.

Space rocks had always fallen on the planet, some more destructive than others, and intermittent periods of intense volcanic activity had created greenhouse effects which had also led to some mass extinctions, but the asteroid that landed so recently on the northern continent, and all its volcanic consequences, had clearly wreaked more havoc than any previous catastrophe. This became even more evident to Nöé as sHe slowly swam hir way northward. As sHe approached to within a thousand miles of the impact crater, the tiny glass beads that had rained down on the surface of the planet soon after the impact, lay thick on the shallow ocean bed like an iridescent mirror.

Unrecognized by the surviving creatures on this devastated world was the intense psychic shock created by the cosmic collision. The *Rock Devas,* with whom Nöé had already formed a warm musical relationship, were the least disturbed, since they seemed to have an innate understanding of cosmic violence. But even their songs had acquired a new and maudlin tone. The *Nature Spirits* themselves were not directly affected by the physical fallout, since they had been warned in good time by their superiors to step back into the safety of their own dimension. However, when they returned to nurture the new growth, their confidence was severely dented by the devastated world they found languishing all around them.

Nöé understood how vital it was that the orderly processes of evolutionary development needed to continue if sHe was eventually to succeed in hir mission. Whether or not the computers had predicted the asteroid's impact, sHe had no memory of having been briefed about it; or, indeed, told how to react if such an event was to occur. SHe knew she had no choice but to allow hir deeper instincts to take over, and hope that all sHe had absorbed in hir long cosmic odyssey would spontaneously coalesce into songs that would encourage and support emerging life. Focusing on this intuition, Nöé moved hir consciousness aside and let the deepest revelations of hir ancient culture pour through hir in wave after wave of melody that echoed over the wasted landscape, the subtle harmonics stroking the dormant life force wide awake again.

The undifferentiated
consciousness of the
planetary
life forms

was similar to
the bonding
Nöé had known
with Hir own race.

However,
by now a new
phenomenon
had appeared.

A small mammalian entity, a lemur of sorts, had yielded a whole plethora of differing life forms, each mutation groping for its own part in biological history.

It was out of this genetic family, that a biped emerged of remarkable courage and great curiosity. Some deep instinct, or was it a future memory.

Over the millions of years following the impact of the asteroid Nöé circled the planet many times, singing hir songs and observing the continents as they spread out in their continuing slow procession across the globe. After a brief respite, the bitter cold that had been a direct result of the fallout from the collision had led to a long period of glaciation, as the great southern continent iced over.

Nöé, as all Helianx, had developed the ability to control hir bodily temperature within certain limits. It had allowed the Helianx to place themselves in states of suspended animation while crossing those interminable interstellar distances. However, with the continents moving steadily apart, and magma pouring up from the oceanic trenches heating the surrounding water, Nöé surprisingly chose to spend more of hir time in the warmer equatorial regions. From that vantage point, sHe was able to take short exploratory trips to both the northern and southern land masses to scrutinize the reemergence of widely differing life forms for the signs that sHe had been waiting for so patiently.

Ice ages came and went; glaciers crept across the land gouging great valleys in their path before retreating back to the polar continents. There were long periods when the planetary climate stabilized and the life force exploded with new forms, many of which would disappear with the next radical climate change. Coming from a world where evolution had been a much simpler affair, Nöé was continually spellbound by the profusion and variety of biological life. This had also been confusing, since the computers had never defined exactly which evolutionary tree would ultimately yield the species of interest to the Helianx. On two or three occasions Nöé had even convinced hirself that a particular species was the one to watch, only to find some global calamity soon drove them to extinction.

Life in the oceans, however, had taken an interesting turn. Some of the large land mammals had chosen--and in some cases were forced by limited access to food--to return to the seas. This had proved to be not only a good survival strategy, since the oceans had always been a far richer source of sustenance than the land, but it had allowed them, over time, to develop some unusual traits. Nöé watched with interest as mutations in this order of life, now known as Cetacea, occurred at a remarkable rate. The buoyancy of the water permitted almost limitless growth, as their bodies became streamlined and their limbs adapted to life in the waters. Fur, now more of an impediment to swift movement, dropped away to be replaced by layers of blubber. Their original tails divided into a pair of flukes, their hind legs disappeared and their forelegs turned into flippers.

Within another few million years there were over 80 different species of whales and dolphins inhabiting almost all the seas and oceans of the planet. Some even grew to a size comparable to the proportions to which Nöé had by now shrunk hirself. But, more importantly, some were growing large and complex brains--and that could only be of interest to the Helianx.

A small mammalian entity – a lemur of sorts – had yielded a whole plethora of differing life forms, each mutation groping for its own part in biological history.

It was out of this genetic family that a biped emerged of remarkable courage and great curiosity.

Some deep instinct, or was it a future memory...

...whispered to the Helianx that this mutation would be the one to watch.

Emerging from an aquatic background Nöé felt a natural affinity for most oceangoing species. With very few exceptions, biological life on every planet the Helianx had charted invariably needed water to nurture and support its existence. Just as the DNA principle, with minor variations, appeared to be common to all life in the universes of space and time, so also were the same basic chemicals involved in the building blocks of life. Water was one, for example, which the Helianx had believed to be the sole possession of Womb Planet, before their planet-hopping explorations had revealed otherwise. Whether it was carried in the bodies of comets, or locked into polar ice; whether rising as steam from swamps, or falling as rain; water, that subtle dance of two hydrogen atoms with one of oxygen, in one form or another, had turned out to be ubiquitous. While the Helianx had not visited every inhabited planet in the vastness of the Multiverse, in their experience, where there was water, there was, or soon would be, life.

As more tens of millions of years passed, Nöé concentrated on tailoring hirself more comfortably to the scale of other creatures in the oceans. Although sHe preferred to spend hir time with hir own tiny clan, sHe found a certain amount of kinship with the large-brained whales. Sometimes sHe even shared in their baleful songs, harmonizing with them and adding layers of tonal meaning that both mystified and entranced the whales. Many of the cetacean species by this point had developed fairly sophisticated echolocation systems with which they were able to find their prey in murky water. This led naturally to their discovery that the sounds generated by their biosonar could be modulated to contain meaning.

But before a complex language was able to evolve, the more sensitive amongst them found that images would spontaneously form in their minds when they communicated with one another. Soon they became more adept at controlling these images, forming and shaping them by manipulating the sound waves. Out of these developments came a rudimentary form of visual telepathy, which allowed a number of the cetacean species to create, over time, mature and benign communities.

Nöé noticed that as the cetacean culture flowered, it seemed to act as a beacon, attracting the attention of other curious extraterrestrial races. Most stayed briefly. After observing the generally primitive state of the land-based species, and not wanting to interfere with the orderly progress of evolution, they moved silently on to other worlds more suited to their needs. There was a small group of aquatic beings, however, who came from a planet in the *Sirius Star System*, and who appeared to Nöé to have a remarkable kinship with some of the smaller species of cetaceans. This extraterrestrial race became regular visitors, reappearing every few millennia to help and guide their cetacean cousins in the ways of the Multiverse.

Yet for all this interplanetary interest, Nöé understood intuitively that it was not going to be the whales or dolphins with whom sHe was to consummate hir secret mission.

...whispered to the Helianx
that this mutation would be
the one to watch.

Life on the continental land masses continued to be a challenging affair, as climatic conditions varied wildly between the periods of glaciation, the ice sheets driving all the creatures towards the warmer equatorial regions; and other times of intense vulcanism, when entire islands of magma, almost overnight, emerged steaming from the ocean. The continuing climatic turbulence was not a welcoming prospect for Nöé.

Although Nöé's preference was to spend most of hir time swimming in the seas which covered the greater part of the planet, sHe made sure to take regular exploratory flights over the grasslands and jungles to see how land-based life was progressing. With the extinction of the large reptiles so many millions of years earlier. Nöé had found hirself continually surprised at the way the mammals simply took over the ecological niches left by the dinosaurs. Many species of mammals had grown very large by this time and although they never reached the proportions of the dinosaurs, the predators amongst them were every bit as fierce as the reptiles, and considerably more cunning.

Nöé's vastly diminished size by now made hir more vulnerable to these large beasts, forcing hir up into the safety of the treetops. It was there, high in the canopy one early evening, and just after the sun had set, that sHe had first spotted the small creature which had so excited hir interest. Bright eyes, full of intelligence and set in a small furry face, had peered out from around a tree branch, before slipping back into the gathering darkness. But not before Nöé had felt a palpable glow of recognition rising in hir heart. Whether or not the little lemur had experienced a reciprocal emotion, Noé doubted, but when sHe pondered the event later, sHe could recall only calm curiosity in those large, reflective eyes.

Not quite believing what hir intuition was telling hir, Nöé continued to keep watch on what had turned out to be a small clan of these creatures. They nested, clustered together in the canopy and seldom, if ever, climbed down to the ground. Appearing to be most active at night, they fed on anything they could get their little claws on. In their favor, Nöé had noted they were quite capable of acting collaboratively on the rare occasion when they were threatened by one of the large cats. Nimbly jumping from branch to branch, they had lured the much larger animal into the higher reaches of the canopy, until the predator, half-hypnotized by hunger, became overconfident, and leapt onto a branch that splintered beneath the animal's weight, plunging it to its death.

Once Nöé had satisfied hirself that this species would be the one to watch, and was pondering hir next movements, sHe suddenly recalled the computers' warning that although sHe might be tempted, sHe was to make sure to involve hirself as little as possible with the natural course of events. The evolutionary process, unique to this experimental world, had to be allowed to unfold with a minimal amount of influence from an external, and unanticipated, source.

Or, at least, until Nöé made hir move.

Time passed,
and evolution continued
in its own
discontinuous
way.
Nöé noticed rapid
and radical changes
befalling the by-now
increasingly
uppity bipeds.

Their brains had swollen into
huge prefrontal cortices
and what small amount of
empathic contact
once possible, the Helianx
now found diminishing.

The bipeds appeared to be
forming, each, an individualized
consciousness...

Nöé's discovery of the lemur community triggered in hir a renewed sense of excitement. SHe had spent so much time on the planet, even for a Helianx, that sHe had started to wonder whether this encounter would ever take place. Hir relief, too, was profound and sHe had to resist a strong urge to observe and nurture this precious find, and to be available to protect them should danger ever seriously threaten them. The lemurs had seemed so small and fragile. Chasing these thoughts out of hir mind, Nöé retreated once again back into the welcoming ocean.

More millions of years passed. The continents continued in their inexorable movement, inching their way to their current positions. Mountain ranges sprung up as tectonic plates collided. Shock waves intermittently rippled around the planet when volcanoes erupted in massive explosions. Ice sheets periodically advanced from the poles, lowering the sea levels and cooling the waters before retreating once again, leaving ravaged landscapes in their trail.

Noë, remembering the computers' admonition, restricted hirself to an occasional short flight over the land, making sure to observe the emerging bipeds from a distance. Groups of these *aquatic apes* hugged the sea shores and river estuaries of the warmer regions, grubbing for shell fish and bobbing and diving in the shallow waters. Nöé noted how spending their lives in and out of sea had allowed these apes to spend more and more of their time upright on their hind legs, which in turn, had freed up their front limbs for more effective foraging. SHe was also astonished at the rapid growth of their brains, fed, as sHe had discovered, by the *Omega-3 fatty acids* sHe knew to be so richly present in the marine food chain.

Nöé intuitively understood that this was a group upon which sHe should keep surreptitious eyes. Other slightly different primates, now down from the trees, had spread out over the savannas, mixing and crossbreeding with yet other primates, and following the seasons and the migrations of the game. As their numbers grew, clans and then tribes had arisen, ferociously defending their territory and venturing further and further into the comparative safety of uninhabited hinterlands. An ever-curious species, they rapidly expanded to every habitable region they could reach, sometimes crossing land-bridges to find entirely new unexplored territories beyond. But, as Nöé well knew, it had not been easy.

Nöé watched nervously as mass extinctions wiped out whole populations, diseases would sometimes run unchecked through an entire tribe, decimating it; famines had struck, challenging the creatures--when not killing them--to find new sources of food. Different nomadic groups had clashed, doing their best to exterminate one another; and most disturbing for Nöé, it seemed that of all the mammals on this richly endowed planet, these particular primates were by far the most vulnerable. Not equipped with venom, tooth or claw, they had only their cunning and their willingness to act collaboratively. And although they appeared to live most of their short lives in a state of constant fear, Nöé was relieved to see that they were also capable of great courage.

...which cut them off from most other undifferentiated life on the planet.

And, this was not the bipeds only problem.

They had been plagued recently by the last-ditch efforts of the remnants of a previous epoch concealed now beneath the thin disguise of godhood...

To terrify them into submissive service.

A strong affinity clearly existed between the extraterrestrial visitors from Sirius and some of Nöé's cetacean friends. Certain tribes of dolphins had long sung of the epic journeys their forebears had taken to a water planet in the Sirius system as proof of kinship. Some of these extraterrestrial *Nommo* had even chosen to stay for longer periods, developing small colonies in the waters around isolated islands in the southern ocean. Nöé had also heard rumors that a group of Nommo were planning cautious contact with carefully selected tribes of bipeds in the heart of one of the great southern continents.

The arrival of the Nommo must have acted as a signal to other aliens, because it seemed to Nöe that the planet had suddenly become intense interest to a steady stream of off-world visitors. Most came and made some brief exploratory trips before slipping away in their silver ships. Others must have found something they valued, because they would stay longer, setting up encampments in the most inaccessible regions.

Nöé was amused to observe a small group hailing from a planet they called Itibi-Ra, who had settled in the jungles of one of the southern continents and were cultivating a particularly toothsome fruit. This they would then harvest and send back to their planet as a much-valued delicacy. Yet other extraterrestrials must have found something of more significant value, because they started elaborate mining operations in another of the vast southern continents.

Nöé watched all this from a distance, cautiously sending out a telepathic tendril every once in a while to check the progress and intentions of the various different groups. Most of them respected the noninterference policy of the local universe authorities, and made sure to camouflage their activities from the indigenous natives. In the unlikely event that their labors were exposed, it was a simple matter to terrify the already fearful locals with a little technological sleight-of-hand and a casual show of power.

There were other groups, more aggressive by nature, who would argue later in MA's civil courts that since the planet was deemed experimental, they could justify their involvement as part of that experiment. But, as Nöé had observed with horror, one of these groups had gone so far as to tamper with the genetic make-up of some of the bipeds, and had then enslaved them to work in their gold mines. Surely, sHe thought, this went way beyond any level of contact that could be considered permissible and yet it appeared to be allowed to continue. Although sHe was appalled at the brutal enslavement, sHe also found hirself encouraged that nothing had been done by the authorities to immediately halt the genetic experimentation. After all, hir own presence on the planet might well be considered illegal under a strict reading of the law and who knew how MA would ultimately rule on hir business on this improbable world.

In the briefing, the computers had impressed on Nöé that what sHe was being required to accomplish would probably be seen by some at MA as being in violation of one of the most fundamental directives of the nonintervention policy. But, they had assured hir with a barely concealed electronic chuckle, if sHe managed to remain undetected until sHe had completed hir mission, then there was not much that MA could do about it, was there?

To terrify them into submissive service.

The bipeds were evolving rapidly while Nöé's attention had been taken by the activities of the extraterrestrial visitors. SHe had managed to remain undetected as much through hir own guile as for the fact that sHe was so much part of the landscape by that time that the visitors appeared to ignore hir on those rare occasions hir guard had slipped.

Although sHe had watched the extraterrestrial comings and goings with interest, Nöé was also pressingly aware that hir main concern needed to be with the indigenous life-forms and how the bipeds were developing.

The mutation that was to lead to the first true humans appeared suddenly as a pair of twins, a male and a female, in a family of mature apes. Even as babies the mutants had looked different to their bewildered primate parents, but since they smelled familiar they were accepted and nurtured to young adulthood. With their considerably larger brains, the young humans' range of mental and emotional responses were so much wider and deeper than their parents that it had not been long before they had struck out on their own, seeking out others of like mind. Nöé had not observed this for hirself, but sHe knew enough about the process of transformation, and how significant mutations can occur within one or two generations, to have some sympathy for the parents of those mysterious and precocious offspring.

Soon enough, a complex language had grown up between increasing numbers of these new humans as they started to gather in clans, and then in larger tribes. While their primate forbears had communicated largely through grunts, roars and body language, their mutated progeny were rapidly able to share with each other what they had learned. This cooperation led to more efficient hunting techniques. The pooling of knowledge on edible plants meant healthier and longer lives; tribal life supported larger families and a natural division of labor allowed for specialization and the development of new and more effective tools.

Over the next half-a-million years, Nöé watched quietly as human beings expanded to all the habitable regions they could reach. With their higher intelligence, they quickly disposed of the more primitive tribes that stood in their way. When different groups of these nomadic humans encountered each other, they either fought bitterly, or were forced into diplomatic truces. Interbreeding between the clans, when it could occur, fed further interesting genetic variations which, in turn, led to yet more ingenious applications of intelligent thought.

But intelligence also had its drawbacks. Already a fearful species, the humans' newly acquired consciousness had profoundly deepened their capacity to imagine the worst. Ghosts and demons now seemed to lurk in the darkness, haunting their dreams and leading to superstitions designed to placate their ravenous needs. Still largely dominated by their animal natures, these early humans were all too readily controlled by the manipulations of the more interfering off-world visitors.

No good can come from this, thought Nöé, as sHe mulled over hir options.

Well the old gods had grown increasingly panicky,

on they found their powers of control diminishing,

Whatever hir apparent concerns Nöé need not have worried. Other forces of which sHe was not aware were slowly grinding into action. The celestial bureaucrats on the capital planet of the *Local Universe* had taken note of this emergent intelligence and had petitioned their superiors for permission to proceed with a legitimate intervention, as time-honored tradition required. This mission was a standard procedure on all inhabited worlds and was slated to occur when the beings on the planet had evolved to a level of intelligence at which they would appreciate help from the outside. Always a tricky business Nöé thought, especially on a world as unrelentingly hostile as this one.

Once the petition for the mission was granted, 100 volunteers with previous experience in planetside life were carefully chosen and prepared; material bodies would need to be genetically tailored for them to thrive under planetary conditions, and an appropriate location for their settlement had to be decided.

After being deposited on Earth in a fertile region near the Persian Gulf, the volunteers, a small group of humanoid intraterrestrials--50 male and 50 female--were to build a teaching center that was later to become the first great city. From there, they were to invite telepathically the most developed individuals amongst the indigenous tribes to come to the city. Living with this group of intraterrestrials, the natives would then learn new approaches to agriculture and animal husbandry, to social relationships and appropriate technology, and then return to their people with all that they had picked up. In this way, the local authorities could ensure a gradual upstepping of consciousness at the same time as allowing the natives the important awareness that they were not alone in the Multiverse.

Although Nöé was broadly aware of the administrative structure of the Multiverse, the computers had not briefed hir in detail as to what to expect from the local authorities. In spite of all hir ancient wisdom and hir telepathic skills sHe had no immediate dimensional access to the inner worlds of the celestial government, and as a consequence had given them little thought until the day this small band of volunteers had arrived and set up camp.

Nöé did not witness the disembarkation, since sHe was basking in the ocean on the other side of the planet at the time. It was only when sHe reached out one of hir telepathic tendrils that sHe caught a brief sense of another kind of intelligence on the planet. SHe had quickly withdrawn, hoping that hir presence had remained undetected, and then started on the long swim around the planet to where sHe had located the source of the signal.

Stopping every once-in-a-while to rest, Nöé cautiously projected sensitive telepathic feelers to scope out this new set of visitors. Soon sHe discovered that although they had definitely originated off-world, compared to the other extraterrestrials sHe had observed coming and going over the millennia, this group appeared to Nöé to be remarkably unsophisticated. Their telepathic reach, for example, appeared to be limited to a few hundred miles and they showed no signs of being aware of hir. More significantly, however, from what Nöé could discern, the visitors were settling in to make themselves a permanent presence on the planet.

Contemporary cosmologists can now more fully appreciate the dynamics that were starting to polarize opinion between the bureaucrats in the *Local System Headquarters*. What was to flower a quarter-of-a-million years later into a full-scale rebellion amongst the celestials was still only a whispered general discontent. So, perhaps it can be said the seeds of the dissent that had arisen later between the visitors, or the *Prince's Staff*, to call them what they called themselves, had already been laid down by the time they arrived. And did they but know it, a pattern of rebellion and violence was created within the psychosphere of the planet which rippled down through time, and that would deeply trouble all future generations as well as the off-planet missions.

However, there were few signs of this discontent on the surface, as the visitors settled into their busy life on this strange new world. Having arrived in the waters within sight of the town that was growing fast with a stream of helpers drawn from the natives, Nöé decided to keep hir distance. When sHe realized that the visitors appeared to be focused on their building project to the exclusion of all else, sHe gained the confidence to wriggle closer to the brick walls of the town. There sHe found a massive tree, its crown lofted above the forest canopy, from where sHe could keep a watchful eye on the visitors and what they were doing.

The Prince's Staff, in their turn, happily unaware of Nöé's presence, continued in their task of doing their best to upgrade human life. It was clearly a long and tedious process. Even the most intelligent of the natives seemed to be consumed with fear and although the visitors tried to show kindness towards them whatever the provocation, the contact between the two species became increasingly frustrating. There were some individual exceptions, of course, but even those courageous souls, when they were returned to their kin, frequently were killed by their terrified tribe. Those who survived did so through their own cunning and often became the shamans of their people--the intermediaries between human beings and the realm of the spirits.

Regardless of the slow-going, the passing millennia saw a gradual global transformation. New approaches to health and child-rearing had ensured rapid increases in population and the introduction of agriculture had led first to settlements, and then to towns. The visitors taught their students the arts of brick-making, which proved to be very popular and subsequently encouraged an era of city-building. Clustering people together in this way produced a need for new social relationships. The primacy of tribal connections soon evaporated when individuals from previously hostile clans found more profit in dealing fairly with one another. Genocidal wars that had characterized the time before the arrival of the Prince's Staff became of less compelling interest, as the civilizing influence of the visitors took hold. Advances in boat-building also allowed the more adventurous amongst the humans to cross hitherto impassable waters and to spread over unpopulated continents. The planetary upgrade appeared to be developing in time-honored and orderly fashion. Yet Nöé, telepathically sensitive to the emotional well-being of the visitors, detected subtle signals that under the surface all was not well. As for Nöé's by-now numerous deceased offspring, their enormous skeletal remains settled into the earth or the seabed, often becoming fossilized, creating the bedrock of the planet's sacred landscape.

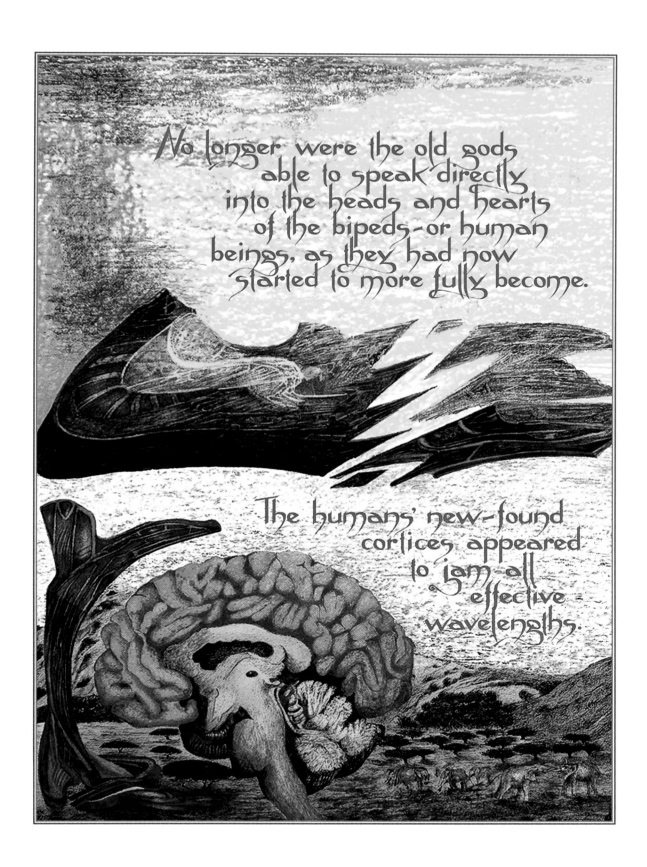

No longer were the old gods able to speak directly into the heads and hearts of the bipeds - or human beings, as they had now started to more fully become.

The humans' new-found cortices appeared to jam all effective wavelengths.

When news of the celestial rebellion finally filtered down to the Prince's Staff, it confirmed for many of them what had become increasingly worrying about the nature and quality of their own lives on the planet. What were they really doing there? Why was so much time and attention spent trying to civilize an unruly and pigheaded species on a small insignificant world far from the center of the action? Why did there have to be so many restrictions on what they were, and were not, able to do? Surely they should be considered mature enough by now to take matters into their own hands and not have to constantly refer back to their superiors for every decision?

More confident now in hir telepathic eavesdropping, Nöé listened fascinated as the arguments amongst the visitors grew more heated. Differences soon became irreconcilable, some holding loyally to their cultural mission, whilst the majority of others, sensing new freedoms in the air, decided to strike out on their own. Territories were claimed, and then fought over. Terrible new weapons were introduced by the rebel groups. The reduced number of loyalists were forced to defend themselves, while at the same time attempting to continue with their original mission.

Nöé watched silently as the situation rapidly deteriorated. No longer was it just the most evolved humans who were drawn to work with the Prince's Staff, but with the rebellion, there were suddenly a number of superhuman beings distributed around the face of the planet, who clearly took pleasure in terrifying the already superstitious, and completely unprepared, local natives. Wars once again ripped through the human populations, now incited by the competing rivalries of the godlike beings who dominated their lives. The high intentions of those who remained true to their mission dissipated over time as the loyalists amongst the Prince's Staff struggled to control an increasingly chaotic situation.

It should be added, for a fuller appreciation of this sad interlude in early human affairs, that by the time of the rebellion, the Prince's Staff had been considerably enlarged by the progeny of their unions. Some of these puzzling offspring, known later as *Midwayers*, were even invisible to the human eye--although, fortunately, not to Nöé's sensitive perceptions. These highly intelligent creatures were almost all swayed by the talk of freedom. A large number of them aligned themselves with the rebel factions, acting effectively as espionage agents, since they were able to mix unobserved with opposition forces.

Nöé made a mental note that it was the ability of these mysterious agents to move in and out of the ultraviolet range of frequencies, which allowed them to appear and disappear at will, that had provoked such awe in these fearful and superstitious people, and that had left them so sadly vulnerable to exploitation.

This was nothing that Nöé had anticipated, or indeed, had ever been warned about, in hir original briefing. Coming from a peace-loving race--personal violence never having been practiced by the Helianx--sHe was continually astonished and horrified by the irrational ferocity of the battling tribes and the ease with which the humans were manipulated by the visitors and their invisible henchmen.

On top of that, the humans were starting to think for themselves and that could only mean trouble.

Plans for a race of subservient robots were crashing around the old gods' feet, dashed by cortical independence.

As a last straw -- by now safely out of the trees -- were starting to dig up, cut down, and consume all manner of power plants which exploded in their brains with visions of their own godhood.

Many thousands of years passed as the original mission of the Prince's Staff, in spite of the courageous attempts of the loyalists, descended into internecine struggles, and ultimately, into chaos. The rebel factions discovered that by posing as gods and goddesses, they were able to more effectively manipulate human actions and intentions. The revelation, originally delivered by the Prince and his Staff, of a single Creative Spirit whose Hand lay behind all of Creation, became lost in the more immediate claims and demands of those posing as divinities. Fear of the unknown, coupled with what appeared to Nöé to be a hard-wired instinct to worship what was powerful and what they did not understand, left the humans particularly exposed to the machinations of the rebels.

As the situation amongst the Prince's Staff had spun further out of control, it was obvious to Nöé that the humans themselves were changing. The challenges posed by the web of constantly shifting rivalries between these renegade factions had driven the humans, through a perverse sort of natural selection, to higher levels of functional intelligence. This appeared to Noe to accompany an increase in individuation which, over time, gradually closed them off to the telepathic demands of these quasi-divinities.

Other calamities had also befallen the Prince's Staff as a result of the Prince's decision to throw in his lot with the celestial rebellion. Since the central issue was one of freedom, the local Multiverse Authorities responded by simply giving the rebels what they wanted, and had subsequently isolated from the larger Multiverse context all the 37 worlds aligning themselves with the rebellion. Extraterrestrial visitors were to be much more carefully monitored; celestial intervention was to be minimized to the absolutely essential; and the offending worlds were left to work out matters on their own.

More unfortunate, however, for the original 100 Prince's Staff--the ones with the humanoid bodies--was MA's decision to selectively filter out some of the incoming cosmic rays. The staff's extreme personal longevity was dependent on a complex electrochemical interaction in their bodies that was promoted by just these cosmic energies. It was a bitter realization of failure. Unable to sustain themselves, one by one, loyalist and rebel alike, whatever had been each ones' expressed belief, had fallen ill over time, and had died.

Their offspring, the Midwayers, not reliant on the energies that sustained their parents, lived on over the generations of humanity to enter history as the divine pantheons of the ancients. Cultures rose and fell, as different gods and goddesses gained ascendence, then overreached, only to be replaced by another set of power-hungry and ambitious self-proclaimed divinities. Great civilizations blossomed briefly and then dissolved in a series of planetary disasters. Massive earthquakes swept entire islands into the ocean; volcanic eruptions buried ill-placed cities in rivers of molten rock; famine and disease, in spite of all the prayers to the various deities, continued to sweep unabated through the human races. These were dark times for the planet so carefully chosen by the Helianx as the one, hopefully, that would ensure their eventual survival.

As a last straw,
the humans—by now
safely out of the trees—
were starting to
dig up, cut down, and
consume all manner
of power plants,
which eploded in their
brains with visions
of their own godhood.

When the Multiverse Authorities discern that a planet has reached a stage of development at which the civilizing effects of the Prince's mission were intended to have taken root, and the indigenous natives would have lost some of their animal belligerence, then MA decides to send down a second mission. Whereas the first intervention was designed to upgrade humanity through a long period of skillful social engineering, the purpose of the second, almost half-a-million years later, was primarily intended to tweak the genetics of the human races. This was achieved by placing on the planet a pair, a male and a female, of extraordinarily fertile intraterrestrials, with bodies fashioned to cope with the physical conditions of the world in question. Their countless offspring were then planned to interbreed with the indigenous natives, thus introducing into the human genome what MA colloquially called, *Violet Blood.*

Although this was a well-established custom, practiced on all planets harboring intelligent life, Nöé was aware from hir intergalactic adventures that under normal conditions the actions of the local Prince's Staff would have carefully prepared the way for the arrival of the intraterrestrial pair. But this was clearly not a normal planet and despite the efforts of the few who had remained loyal to the dictates of MA to welcome the arrival of the couple, it was a sorry place that greeted them. Tribes of fearful natives, their lives dominated and controlled by thoroughly questionable entities, fought endless wars for the satisfaction of their counterfeit divinities.

Many of the innovations introduced by the Prince's Staff, so many thousands of years earlier, had fallen into disuse, and then had been forgotten. As their time was running out some of the Staff had ignored their superiors, mating illicitly with natives and producing generations of unintended genetic mutations. The city that the Prince's Staff had so lovingly constructed in the early years of their mission had long since sunk under the encroaching waters of the Red Sea, dispersing the survivors to make their own way in the world.

So, instead of finding a neat, well-organized world on their arrival, the two intraterrestrial botanists were met with chaos and all the challenges posed by the evident failure of the previous mission. Nöé was probably the only being on the planet who was wholeheartedly delighted to register their presence. Making sure to stay well outside the pair's telepathic reach, sHe was able to sense them trying to settle into their new home on a fertile peninsular projecting into one of the smaller of the central seas. Thus, Nöé was able to drift close to the shore, while still remaining undetected.

Silently sHe watched these two beautiful individuals--and for such large, ungainly creatures, all Helianx possessed a surprisingly fine aesthetic sense--as the couple attempted to encourage their small band of dispirited companions. Each of the pair was almost twice as tall as the largest of the natives and yet to Nöé's eyes, both were elegantly proportioned with long, slim, limbs, golden skins tanned by the sun, and the bluest of eyes in their open, innocent faces.

To Nöé subtle perceptions, the glorious pair appeared to glow with health and were surrounded by a shimmering violet aura.

Nöé withdrew back into the open ocean in deep thought. The computers had touched on this second off-world mission, but only to tell Nöé that the event would act as a signal hir moment was fast approaching. Now, as sHe recalled the briefing, sHe could remember nothing more of significance being said, apart from the generalities that held true for all planetary missions of biological upliftment.

In their extensive intergalactic travels the Helianx had made a point of not revealing themselves to any planetary population in the early stages of their evolution. The Space Gypsies were able to assess from their out-of-the-body observations at what point a world's people had reached in its progress towards settlement in Light and Life, and this had allowed them to avoid even a hint of unauthorized interference.

If there was one thing that all intelligent species have learned on their own planets in their long struggle towards peaceful coexistence, it would have to be the need to exercise considerable caution whenever a more developed culture has stumbled on a less evolved one. They would have observed for themselves the negative impact of their presence on the more primitive of their own peoples, since early planetary populations are invariably composed of different races, often endowed with very different abilities.

In the relatively rare event of a space-faring race encountering a world at a more primitive stage of development, the protocols of engagement forbidding any direct contact always held true unless specifically sanctioned by MA. An exception was made only when a particularly belligerent species showed signs of putting its weapons into space, endangering life on nearby planets. In those cases it was regarded as perfectly permissible to disable the threatening technology. In fact, it had become something of an amiable competition between different interested parties to come up with original, and often humorous, ways of confusing and mystifying the warlike race in question before it could do any real damage.

Fortunately, the immense distances of interstellar space and the relatively short life-spans of most species ensured that only the most mature races were able to develop the capability of interplanetary travel. Whatever technology was used, the enormous commitment of time and resources required to develop a craft capable of traversing these distances, invariably spoke of many generations of peaceful cooperation and shared intention. Of course, there were some rare exceptions to this; warrior species seeking to dominate, or colonize, nearby planets, but even on those rare occasions when they were permitted to leave their planet, there is no record of them ever being able to travel outside their solar systems.

When an authorized intervention, such as that attempted by the Prince's Staff, had resulted in such unintended and difficult consequences, MA regarded this as a tacit warning to the increasing number of off-planet races who had become suddenly very interested in this world. Celestial uprisings were so infrequent in a benign and well-regulated Multiverse, that the act of isolating rebellious planets was bound to produce some unexpected and intriguing transformations in the indigenous populations.

For Nöe, too,
at this point in Hir evolution,
having become a rather magnificent,
but manageable, plumed serpent,
the day of reckoning
was fast
approaching;

the point at which the Helianx
might bind Hir karma to
that of the humans
so that a successful
cross-species mating
could take place.

The day started innocently enough with Nöé coiled entrancingly around a large and friendly tree, taking in the morning sun.

Many changes, too, had been shaping the human races over this last crucial few hundred thousand years of their development. The demands of survival and the challenging climatic conditions had triggered the mutations required to cope with a wide variety of difficult circumstances. Diets changed as more efficient weapons made hunting larger animals possible, and this in turn contributed the protein needed for bigger brains and stronger bodies. Whole nomadic populations became trapped on the great northern continent as the ice receded. Sea levels rose behind them, forcing them to adapt to frigid new conditions. By this time groups of *Neanderthals* had developed remarkably large brains, and yet isolated from the innovations introduced by the Prince's Staff, they had not progressed much beyond living in caves and using simple stone implements.

In the more temperate regions, a *Cro-Magnon* subspecies had emerged from the proto-human line as the dominant mutation. It was from this group that the Prince's Staff, in their heyday, chose those individuals to educate and then send back to their own people to share all they had learned. Complex languages had started to emerge, which both deepened relationships and made the transmission of knowledge between generations more effective. With all this new knowledge came power and confidence, which in turn led to elaborate social hierarchies replete with kings, standing armies, aristocracies, accumulated wealth and the traditions of priestcraft.

Almost all the closely-held metallurgical secrets brought by the Prince's Staff had been lost in the destruction of their city. The Staff had always made sure to keep the sophisticated technology they used for constructing their antigravity vehicles well out of the sight of curious natives. Inevitably, this had led to their craft being worshipped as divine apparitions on the rare occasions they had been seen. Most of these skills had melted away, however, when the bitter conflict between the staff had driven them apart. Then, as the waves swept over their city and the remnants fled, the highest technical culture the world had yet seen passed into legend. In the ensuing millennia of chaos, unsuccessful attempts had been made to work with tin, or copper, when it could be found in natural outcroppings, but the art of alloying these metals to cast into bronze implements had to be rediscovered much later.

After the long, slow rhythms of the early evolutionary process, Nöé was fascinated to watch how rapidly matters were developing all around hir. The hunting and gathering of nomadic tribes was rapidly becoming replaced by an agricultural economy centered around small villages and market towns. Memories of a legendary city, or perhaps simply the natural tendency for human beings to congregate in the same place, drove yet another era of city-building on every continent that the humans had reached. Civilizations rose, flowered briefly and then collapsed under their own weight, or were overrun by another warlike horde.

In this bewildering panorama of shifting cultures Nöé found it next to impossible to decide how, where, or with whom sHe should consummate hir mission.

The day started innocently enough with Nöé coiled entrancingly around a large and friendly tree, taking in the morning sun.

On the ground far below Nöé overheard the incessant rambling monologue of a Jehovah or was it a Baal?

The loud voice was presumably remonstrating to a couple of poor bewildered humans about eating this and not eating that.

Nöé caught the same old lies that sHe had heard so often before: the boastful pseudo-omnipotence of a strutting dictator.

Contemporary cosmologists have long argued as to the exact point in time at which Nöé decided to modify the plans so carefully prepared for hir by the computers back on the Great Ship. Some have maintained what little documentation still remains clearly suggests that it was at the moment sHe first saw the two intraterrestrial botanists. Others have theorized that such a radical decision must have taken more serious consideration, especially in light of what occurred later.

The truth, as is often the case, was a mixture of both. Nöé had found hirself deeply, and quite unexpectedly, drawn to the magnificent pair at first sight. So much so that sHe had withdrawn reflexively in surprise. Not only were they both a delight to hir eyes, but sHe could sense an intelligence very different from anything sHe had previously encountered on this world. Yet for all hir rising sense of excitement, sHe was more than aware that such a critical change of plan would need to be very carefully considered.

The Midwayers, who had lived on after the death of their parents, especially those who had taken to posturing as local deities, always seemed to Nöé to possess a very limited intelligence. SHe found the demands and limitations they imposed on their vulnerable worshippers became progressively more irrational as time had passed, and worse, that the density of planetary life had thickened the Midwayers' emotional needs and responses. It was just this emotional deterioration in the consciousness of these once brilliant beings that was directly responsible for so much of the ensuing chaos.

Exosociologists who have studied the consequences of celestial rebellions on the worlds affected by such profound upheavals have pointed out that isolating the offending planets, while a sensible policy from the local authority's point of view, because the systemwide quarantine prevented further spread of the dissent, must also necessarily result in severely traumatizing the remaining Midway creatures. With the subsequent death of their parents, they would be bound to feel doubly abandoned and desperate. The sociologists added that this confusion would be compounded if the Prince, as was the case on this planet, succumbed to the temptation of assuming absolute power. In setting himself up as the supreme god of this world, the Prince would have tacitly encouraged the Staff's rebellious offspring to use the mantle of divinity as one of the only effective means left to them in their need to control human beings.

Nöé had watched this unappealing behavior repeat itself wherever these gods and goddesses had gathered. Although in some cases feeble attempts had been made to uplift the natives by playing on their superstitious natures, little had been done to encourage the evolution of a truly independent intelligence. These self-proclaimed deities, while they were emotionally degenerating under the weight of hubris and their own internecine struggles for dominance, had become, over time, all the more dictatorial and demanding of their half-hypnotized flocks, manipulating them through fear and guilt for their own devious and jealous ends.

On the ground far below Nöé overheard the incessant rambling monologue of a Jehovah or, was it a Baal?

The loud voice was presumably remonstrating to a couple of poor bewildered humans about eating this and not eating that.

Nöé caught the same old lies that SHe had heard so often before; the boastful psuedo-omnipotence of a strutting dictator.

Thoughtforms never could get godhood straight-- Nöé thought to Hirself, and sighed a small billow of smoke, then silence.

Nöé had taken hir time in making hir decision, slowly circling the globe and enjoying the freedom of the open oceans--perhaps for the last time. Back at the briefing, the computers had little to say of what was to become of Nöé and hir small clan after sHe had accomplished hir mission. This uncertainty had been exaggerated, as sHe well knew, by the unanticipated event of the celestial rebellion. Although the computers had been aware of a couple of previous uprisings amongst the lower levels of the celestial bureaucracy, these were not thought to have been sufficiently disruptive to have to burden Nöé with any additional strategies designed to deal with such a rare occurrence.

SHe had been well-briefed on the second mission, since the arrival of the botanists was said to be a key sign that hir own mission was nearing its culmination. By this time, and under more normal circumstances, sHe might have expected the human population to be far more advanced in development than were the confused and fearful beings sHe encountered in hir travels around the globe. SHe knew from hir previous Multiverse experience that intervention protocol required the world in question to have been set well in order by the time of the arrival of the second biological mission. And yet here they were, an unfortunate pair, deposited on their verdant peninsular amidst indigenous natives still terrified of their own shadows, and deposited on a small and seemingly insignificant world devastated by constant wars, famines, and extreme climatic conditions.

Not for the first time, Nöé thought that it was all very odd. SHe recalled this was known to be an experimental planet, but that would not fully explain such a radical break with tradition. Something had to be going on behind the scrim of reality and unfortunately for Nöé, sHe had no dimensional access to those realms of celestial organization. Yes, sHe had agreed with hirself, it was very strange; ever since the rebellion had struck, nothing had been even vaguely similar to the picture painted by the computer simulations back on the Great Ship.

The few attempts Nöé had made to communicate with human beings had been notable failures. The humans, accustomed to being oppressed by the cruel demands and bullying antics of their overlords, had proved themselves quite incapable of being in hir presence. Some had run in terror at the first sight of this improbable creature, so gentle and seductive, and yet who seemed to be filling their heads with sound; others had fallen into hopeless fugue states; whilst still others appeared to be possessed by a strange madness, writhing around on the ground and foaming at the mouth, until exhausted they, too, had fallen into a long sleep.

As for the Midway creatures, Nöé had long observed with horror some of the techniques used by those spurious divinities to control their flocks of devotees. By now a class of priests and priestesses had arisen to act as privileged intermediaries, making it possible to continue to manipulate their followers, even as the Midwayers' own voices were fading in the minds of most humans.

Desperate times, thought Nöé, might well require desperate measures.

—Thoughtforms
never could
get godhood
straight—
Nöé thought
to Hirself,
and sighed
a small billow
of smoke…
then silence.

Uncoiling, Nöé slid lazily down the tree to where the humans stood quietly together.

The female, over whom the Helianx cast an appreciative and androgynous glance, was holding in both hands the beautiful reddish-golden cap of a mushroom.

Nöé had not been idle in preparing hirself for the encounter ahead, the epiphany for which sHe had been chosen so carefully and that, one way or another, would seal the fate of hir race. Using hir genetic skills, and working extensively with hir RNA, Nöé had finally reduced hir size to more modest proportions. SHe no longer inspired quite the same automatic response of terror in the few human beings to whom sHe had chosen to quietly reveal hirself. SHe picked carefully, selecting only those with the most independent minds and who had managed to separate themselves from the tyranny of the counterfeit deities. A tradition of using visionary plants had grown up amongst some of the more curious and courageous humans, which had allowed them a far deeper perception of reality and an understanding of the truth unmediated by the manipulations of gods and goddesses, or the priests and priestesses that served them.

Nöé soon found that even those rare individuals who were able to sustain hir presence without running away, often had the unfortunate proclivity of collapsing uselessly into a deep hypnotic trance when the cognitive dissonance grew too extreme. Nöé, as all Helianx, had met with this reaction amongst some species on their interplanetary travels on the rare occasions they had explored a primitive world.

Not having evolved from a predatory past and considering themselves essentially well-meaning by nature, it had always been difficult and frustrating when they had encountered this defensive response. Luckily, as most intelligent species matured, and as they became gradually more accustomed to living in a vast Multiverse populated by strange beings of every shape and size, they grew less threatened by the overwhelming presence of the Helianx.

The situation in which Nöé found hirself this time, however, was rather different. Here, there was no possibility of retreat, of slipping away back into the galactic night, leaving only trace memories in the myths of a terrified planetary population. Here, sHe did not have the luxury of normal levels of Helianx detachment. SHe knew sHe had no choice but to break through the interspecies barrier by whatever means sHe could summon. And not only that: sHe needed to gain the complete trust of those sHe would ultimately choose.

The computers had insisted that there had to be a willing complicity, specifically from the female of the species, if the genetic transference was to be effectively accomplished. Anything less than that would be sure to create a karmic trauma that would echo down through the generations of humanity, forever imprinting the species with an implacable dread of the unknown.

Nöé was all too aware of the terrified reactions sHe evoked whenever sHe had tried to befriend human beings, and it was simply not in hir nature to want to add to their burden of fear. Besides, sHe knew that when the time was right for the eventual expression of the Helianx genetic and historical reality as an inner experience, its emergence was going to be frightening enough without further encumbrances hard-wired into the species through any act of hir desperation.

Uncoiling,
Nöé slid lazily down
the tree to where the humans
stood quietly together.

The female, over whom the
Helianx cast an
appreciative and androgy-
nous glance, was holding
in both hands the
beautiful reddish-
golden cap of
a mushroom.

Nöé was starting to realize that sHe would have to act soon. SHe knew the window of opportunity signaled by the arrival of the two intraterrestrials would not remain open for very much longer. In addition, it was becoming disturbingly obvious to hir that the psychic density of the planet was already wearing down the noble pair's good intentions; as once it had for so many of the late Prince's Staff and their troubled offspring. This constant state of worry was only exacerbated by warring tribes of humans, spurred on by their local deities and their continuing attempts to invade the sanctuary that the botanists had created for themselves.

An expertise in agronomy and the deep knowledge of the biological sciences that the pair brought with them to the planet had led them to cultivate much of their fertile peninsula. They also carefully studied, named and recorded the native flora and fauna in the sophisticated laboratory they had built in their encampment. Making minor genetic modifications to some of the cereal crops and fruit trees growing naturally all around, they were able to refine them, vastly increasing the yield and making them much more resistant to disease. Their work with animals, Nöé had noted, was also producing remarkable results. Whilst many individual humans in the nomadic tribes had formed touchingly close, interdependent relationships with the animals they followed on their migrations, the kinder treatment and the selective breeding programs instituted by the botanists led to both a far higher quality of produce, and much more contented animals. Creatures that had previously been thought of as wild were tamed, and in some cases even domesticated; others were kept in surprisingly good conditions for their milk and wool. Cattle were no longer slaughtered for their meat, since the scientists were both vegetarians and had demonstrated to their motley little group of followers some of the healthy advantages of not eating animal flesh. Their wide knowledge of terrestrial biology obviated much of the trial-and-error approach that had led to the poisoning of so many hungry, or curious, natives. This had led, in turn, to a far broader and more varied diet.

Anxiously, Nöé had watched from a safe distance as the first few buildings rapidly developed into a small village. With the help of some of the Staff's offspring who had remained loyal to MA's local edicts, together with those few humans who had affiliated themselves with both off-planet missions, the botanists had evidently attempted to recreate something of the paradise they had known before they had volunteered for this increasingly difficult mission.

The city that had grown up around the site of the first mission had long since disappeared under the waves in one of the warmer periods of the planet's climatic history. Had the city continued to flourish under more normal conditions, and had the Prince and his staff not fallen so thoroughly into feuding, the scientists would have been able to build on the developments introduced by the first mission in its almost half-a-million years on the planet. For the two frustrated off-world scientists, however, it was as though they had to start completely afresh, but with the additional hazards of a fearful and traumatized population, and the persistent hostility of so many rebellious Midwayers.

Time for some some straight talk, Nöé thought and SHe sang to the humans one of the oldest and most flamboyant melodies in the Helianx repertoire.

Rondos followed, then a toccata led to the most harmonious of fugues. Concertos were tempered by pastorals and serenades as the effects of the delicious fungus began to take a hold on all present.

After a lot more practice Nöé managed to master a more creative use of hir *chromatophores* to such a point that sHe was able, at will, to send shivers of iridescent color rippling down hir long body. Whereas once sHe had only been able to crudely camouflage hirself against a relatively monochromatic background, sHe had by now developed sufficient micro-muscular control to accompany hir songs with a delightful array of delicately shifting colors. Not possessing lungs in any conventional sense, the numerous vocal chords of a Helianx were connected directly to hir internal buoyancy chambers. Practice allowed hir to match her songs with the rippling play of colors and reflected light.

This had allowed the Helianx feats of extraordinarily vocalization, with complex harmonies intertwining sometimes far beyond the limited range of human hearing. It had also forced Nöé to compress hir songs and retune them to the denser frequencies of terrestrial life. Hir songs, however, although crafted into masterpieces of tonal modulation, and carrying memories of hir race's boundless intergalactic adventures, had meant very little to the apparently tone-deaf humans.

It was this bewildering tumult of sound, issuing mysteriously from a flickering serpentine form curled around the branches of a large tree, that had so confused and frightened the humans, sending them once again into hypnotic, fugue states-of-mind, and making them completely unavailable to hir seductive advances. Try as Nöé might, the result was always the same. SHe had found it very frustrating. But, time was pressing in and a decision had to be made.

Nöé had never felt so alone in all hir many millions of years on the planet. Hir kin, back on the Great Ship, would be tucked into their nutrient pods by now in somnolent states of suspended animation, safely buffered against the massive stresses of gravity, and more significantly, also completely dependent on hir for their survival. The frightful responsibility of what sHe had taken on became more real as sHe contemplated the choice that faced hir. SHe was having absolutely no success with any of the humans sHe had approached, and it was with humans that the computers had insisted sHe should meld. However, it appeared that the computers, so consistently thorough in their analysis, also had their lacunae, since they had evidently made no allowance whatsoever for the dilemma in which Nöé now found hirself.

But then again, as sHe thought more deeply about hir options, sHe pondered whether perhaps those electronic genii had known very well what they were doing. Having observed for hirself the devastating effects of a celestial rebellion, Nöé had found it hard to believe that any reasonable analysis would not have included the ensuing chaos as a very real possibility. No, sHe thought, remembering the emphasis that had been placed on the necessity of meeting the challenges of a dense and problematic planet, the computers must have had their own good reasons for remaining silent on this.

Besides, if sHe had known in advance just how difficult hir mission was going to turn out to be, Nöé wondered whether sHe would have been quite as enthusiastic about taking it on.

Chants
    layered over by
        cantatas;
        ballads,
        arias,
            reels,
            chorales,
                all swept forth,

        until finally,
    a superb nocturne
        shimmered in long
            tendrils of sound
        around the ecstatic humans. —
                The scene was set.

Everything else went much as planned. The Jehovah, for that is who it turned out to be, predictably enough, blundered straight into the trap and condemned the three of them to all manner of hideous and malicious punishments. But not before the artful Heliarxc had consummated Hir replicatory mission with the female in a quiet and majestic orgasm.

The seed was placed.

History, or so Nöé hopes, is taking good care of the rest.

Once Nöé had emerged from hir meditative trance, it became much clearer to hir that sHe needed to throw in hir lot with the newly-arrived botanists. SHe had satisfied hirself on the impossibility of fulfilling hir mission with any of the indigenous humans sHe had encountered. And besides, sHe recalled the warm glow sHe felt when sHe first saw the exquisite pair. Here, at least, were beings who should be able to tolerate hir unlikely presence without fleeing in terror and who, sHe hoped, might even be able to understand the true reason for hir being on the planet. Perhaps sHe could take advantage of the botanists' mission to infuse humanity with a massive infusion of violet blood.

Making hir way into the warmer water of the sea that bordered the coast of the peninsula, Nöé finally reached the gently sloping shoreline and pulled hirself cautiously out of the surf. Pausing briefly on the beach, sHe dried hir long body in the sun. Then, flexing hir small wings, sHe lofted hirself up into the thick canopy of the forest that bordered the seashore. Once up there sHe felt more secure from being seen by someone passing far beneath hir on the forest floor, and it gave hir ample time to effectively camouflage hirself against the mottled greens of the background vegetation. By this time sHe had become so adept at manipulating hir chromatophores that sHe was able to replicate, along the surface of hir body, all the subtle changes in tone and movement of the leaves dappled by beams of sunlight slicing through the canopy.

In hir previous explorations Nöé had taken careful note of the limits of the telepathic reach of the two off-world scientists and had found it a comparatively simple matter to veil hir existence from their psychic awareness. However, sHe had never ventured this far inland before and sHe knew that the closer sHe drew to them, the harder it would be to keep a psychic shield in place. SHe would have to come up with some method of approaching the pair as closely as possible without being perceived as a threat.

Taking hir time, and with this dilemma in mind, Nöé undulated hir long body, moving fluidly through the tree tops as sHe approached closer to the village. From this vantage point sHe was able to appreciate how much progress the botanists had made in spite of all the problems they had to face. The forest had been selectively cleared and small areas planted and carefully tended. SHe could even see open fields in the distance, the golden grasses shimmering in the morning breeze. A herd of large mammals were contentedly chewing on their cud, as they made their slow way down to a nearby stream to drink.

Nöé paused in the crown of a magnificent oak tree and dropping into a light meditation sHe focused hir psychic awareness on the pair. SHe could feel their presence like a faint telepathic tickle in the back of hir mind and realized with a shock that they must be picking up on hir. Probing deeper, sHe started to sense an intensity to their curiosity as they courageously made their way through the trees towards where sHe was perched.

Wrenching hirself out of hir trance Nöé knew with Supreme clarity that hir moment had arrived. This was the point of no return. Now there was no turning back.

Everything else went much as planned. The Jehovah, for that is who it turned out to be, predictably enough, blundered straight into the trap and condemned the three of them to all manner of hideous and malicious punishments. But not before the artful Helianx had consumated Hir replicatory mission with the female in a quiet and majestic orgasm.

The seed was placed.

History, or so Nöé hopes, is taking good care of the rest.

Nöé gathered hir ancient wits about hir and gently propelled hirself forward, sending waves of telepathic reassurance rippling ahead of hir as sHe started hir song. First quietly, like the wind in the trees and the calls of small animals and birds; then, as sHe approached the fascinated intraterrestrial botanists, hir song grew more full and complex as sHe superimposed deeper and deeper layers of meaning on the subtle rhythms, painting psychic pictures with sound in their minds. SHe felt the beautiful pair becoming increasingly entranced as hir songs whirled like aural ectoplasm around their bronzed bodies.

SHe sung of hir ancient connections, of the Helianx and the demise of their planet; of hir race's endless galactic wanderings and its many discoveries; of the Great Ship and hir beloved kin, fast asleep in a state of suspended animation; of the terrible waste of all that knowledge, should sHe fail in hir mission and the Helianx were to die out as a result. SHe sung of hir long exile on this planet and all the massive changes sHe had witnessed: the comings and goings of the ice sheets; the tragic die-offs and the sudden mutations; massive volcanic eruptions that darkened the sky for years; earthquakes and asteroids that helped shape the continents; the extraterrestrial colonies that arrived and then departed--or, had disappeared under the waves; the rise of the mammals and the ultimate emergence of human intelligence.

Empathically sensing the couple's interest deepen, Nöé modulated hir song to paint more recent events; the chaotic failure of the previous mission and the inexorable descent into madness of so many of its survivors; of how they were masquerading as gods and goddesses and of their bullying, manipulative ways and how they have held their human followers in a thrall of fear...

Nöé paused momentarily when sHe realized how minimally the scientists had been briefed on the true conditions on the planet. Growing more confident and sensing that the pair had become completely absorbed in hir story, sHe resumed hir song with a crescendo of harmonics as sHe eased hirself closer. Now sHe could see them sitting close and hugging each other in a forest glade, a single beam of sunlight turning their fair hair into a golden tangle. They were beautiful creatures--the very apogee of bipedal development. Sitting tall and straight, with muscular, bronzed bodies and a nobility of bearing that even Nöé, of a very different species, found unexpectedly moving. Having kept the pair under telepathic observation since their arrival, Nöé was quite aware of the difficulties the scientists were facing. In the light of this, and what must be the high strangeness of hir own unusual presence, sHe could only admire their serenity. Now the three of them were in the clearing together bathed in soothing golden sunlight. Nöé sinuous body sparkled with iridescence as sHe slowly circled the beautiful pair, drawing them closer into hir ecstatic embrace, while hir winnowing song hung in the air weaving a sequence of hallucinatory visions in the minds of the entranced couple.

Nöé rejoiced in their complete lack of fear, reveling in their delicious, welcoming sexuality. SHe loved their obvious intelligence and their open, honest hearts. In those moments sHe knew sHe had made the right decision and that whatever lay in the future, hir race's destiny would be inextricably and intimately involved with the fate of these two beings. And, of course, their children, and their childrens' children, even until this world is settled in Light and Life.

Certain contemporary metaphysicians have noted that although the legends circulating around the Western world for the last 40,000 years have spoken of Nöé's intervention as a seminal event in human history, the true dynamics of the situation, or, even the real identity of the three participants, have remained largely hidden. And further; that this unlikely encounter should become a simplistic story which painted lurid pictures of the consequences of personal initiative in the face of an angry deity, used by priests and parents to frighten children and extol the virtues of blind obedience, might be explained, in part, by the very complexity of what actually happened.

Human beings, these august savants have argued, have always preferred their myths and legends to make simple points. Something needed to be found to account for the evident woes of the human race. Over time, an endless oral tradition had further simplified the story, placing the emphasis on the consequences of disobedience and the expulsion from paradise of what had become by now the legendary story of the first humans. The talking serpent remained in the saga as a mysterious figure of unexplained origin, who could be blamed conveniently for the downfall of humanity and for sowing the seeds of enmity and deception that have so disastrously influenced human relations down through the centuries.

Although Nöé had successfully completed hir replicatory task and had transferred the Helianx genetic information, now deposited on a cellular level deep within the new host species, the immediate future for all three participants turned out to be far more complicated and troubled than sHe could have anticipated. And yet that, too, had served Nöé's purposes, because within a few centuries the scientists' colony had finally fallen to the ravages of hostile tribes, driving the survivors out into the world to mix and interbreed with the indigenous natives.

Due to this, MA's plan to use the off-world scientists to upgrade and refine the human genetic endowment was severely restricted. As a result of being deprived of this infusion of this violet blood, considered on most worlds to be an essential element in uplifting consciousness in the natural course of evolution of a well-balanced planetary intelligence, humanity became severely shortchanged.

The botanists' mission ultimately came to be seen as a failure and the primary players were withdrawn to Local System Headquarters. This had left the human races--through no fault of their own--once again caught in the middle of the ongoing conflict between seemingly divine entities, growing more crazed by the century and locked endlessly in their battles for dominance. Fertile ground, Nöé realized with a mixture of emotions, for the accelerated evolution of a species that would emerge, in time, as courageous, wise and independent. Human beings who eventually will access, and express, the stream of this ancient race's genetic information, and work with this revelation to complete the final phase of the mission to join and reawaken the Helianx in the Great Ship.

And Nöé slept.

The Rainbow Serpent at the White House: Canyon de Chelly

Helianthropic Glossary
(terms in order of their use)

Superuniverse: All seven superuniverses are said to circle a Central Universe, which acts as a pattern creation for the many universes of the spacetime continuum. Each superuniverse contains 100,000 Local Universes. *(Urantia Book)*

Multiverse: Used to Include the many dimensions of higher-frequency inner space, from which a vast hierarchy of celestial beings organize the universes of space and time.

Quantum bioengineering: The ability possessed by all Helianx to transmute their biological processes on a cellular level by psychokinetically manipulating sub-electronic particles.

Nanobots: Autonomous organic micro-robots, constructed on a molecular level by the Helianx, to patrol and repair their internal biological circuitry.

Messenger RNA: A nucleic acid polymer which serves as the template for the translation of genes into proteins.

Seeding life: All organic life is said to have been designed and organized within the celestial realms and then downstepped into a planetary dimension to manifest as the natural evolutionary process. *(Urantia Book)*

Mutual symbiosis: The creative interaction between two dissimilar organisms to the advantage of both.

DNA: Deoxyribonucleic acid or deoxyribose nucleic acid is a nucleic acid that contains instructions specifying the biological development of all forms of cellular life. *(Wikipedia)*

Psychomysticism: The study and practice of the psychology of the mystical experience.

Bio-acoustic telepathy: A form of visual telepathy developed by some aquatic species that originally evolved from superimposing and modulating acoustic signals with internally generated visual images.

Cetacea: Order of marine mammals composed of whales, dolphins, and porpoises. Most have exceptionally large brains and reached their optimal stage of physical development some 35-50 million years ago.

Universe Broadcast Circuits: Intelligent life on all inhabited planets are interconnected by an instantaneous transmission system that allows them a developed awareness of the social and political situation in the larger Multiverse context. *(Urantia Book)*

Pervaded and Unpervaded space: Pervaded space can be understood as the horizontal axis of the Multiverse respiratory expansion and contraction. Unpervaded space lies on the vertical axis and is believed to act as a balance to the respiration of the spacetime continuum. *(Urantia Book)*

Eidetic screen: A hypothetical screen within the cranium upon which vivid and detailed mental images can be projected as if actually visible.

Astral energy/astral realms: A nonmaterial realm of existence in which intelligent beings have a paranormal, astral counterpart capable of out-of-the-body travel to the astral regions of other worlds.

Liquid light: A psychokinetic training technology derived from modulating photons into a malleable plasma. It is believed to have been originally developed by an advanced race in the Pleiadean cluster.

Supreme Being: Not a direct Creator, but an evolutionary Deity whose influence expands throughout the Multiverse and will ultimately constitute the collective fusion of experiential power and spiritual personality. *(Urantia Book)*

Celestial collaboration: Intelligent species will frequently seek, and in some cases receive, guidance from celestial beings whose function it is to encourage the orderly progression of evolutionary life.

Emotional body: Many intelligent species possess four contingent and interpenetrating vehicles; the physical, emotional, mental, and spiritual bodies. The latter three subtle bodies both inform, and are developed by, the choices made within the experiential physical realm.

Exopsychology: The study of the psychological processes of intelligent extraterrestrial species.

Telepathic Web: An astral matrix created over time by the constant telepathic activity of the Helianx operating as a collective consciousness.

Psychosphere: The mental and psychic landscape of an individual Helianx, a group of Helianx or the overall psychic atmosphere of an inhabited planet.

First Source and Center: One of the many terms used by different intelligent races in the Multiverse to refer to the Creator.

Spacetime continuum: Includes the physical reality of all seven superuniverses as a subset of the pattern creation of the Central Universe. Also used as a synonym for the universes of time and space.

Thoughtforms: Physical beings capable of intelligent mentation can create, consciously or unconsciously, emotionally powered thoughts that can influence the mental and emotional bodies of other beings.

Uniscan: A subtle energy scanning device developed by the Helianx that registers in wholistic terms the overall development of a planetary species.

Dreamtime: An Australian Aboriginal term for the higher dimensional realms, here used as a colloquial synonym for the astral realms.

Ultimaton: A sub-electronic particle; the smallest possible quanta of matter, one hundred of which are said to vibrate within a single electron. Ultimatons act as tiny white gushers, transducing informational energy from the Central Universe. *(Urantia Book)*

Central Universe: The original pattern Creation from which the universes of time and space are downstepped and in which intelligent beings are endowed with free choice.
(Urantia Book)

Settled in Light and Life: The final epoch of evolutionary attainment in which a global population reaches a level of overall spiritual harmony, social equity, and creative and peaceful cooperation. *(Urantia Book)*

Melchizedek Universities: The great celestial universities, generally based on the architectural worlds of the Local System headquarters and and run by the Melchizedek Brothers.

Melchizedek Brotherhood: an order of high teaching angels. *(Urantia Book)*

Psychohistory: The study of the psychological impact and the effect that the psychology of individuals and groups have on the historical process of an intelligent species.

Psychokinesis: The ability possessed by many advanced races to manipulate objects in consensus reality by mental effort alone.

Local Universe: Each superuniverse supports 100,000 local universes, and each local universe contains ten million inhabited, or inhabitable, planets. Sequentially, our local universe is numbered 611,121 out of the full total of 700,000. Currently, some four million worlds in this local universe are inhabited. *(Urantia Book)*

Beings of the Inner Worlds: Used synonymously with 'celestials' and 'angels' to describe the many orders of beings who administer and officiate over the material universes of time and space.

Serial reincarnation: A spiritual technique in which a soul, or a group of souls, agree to reincarnate in individuals of the same species. This is an exception to most cases where reincarnation is used, in which souls choose to incarnate on different worlds, in physical bodies appropriate for their spiritual growth.

Eugenics: The science and study of improving the genetic, inheritable characteristics of a planetary population by selective breeding.

Corroborree: An Australian aboriginal term for the festive gatherings held when different nomadic tribes cross paths.

Multiverse Administration (MA): A general term for the overall authority in the Multiverse as interpreted by the courts on the various capital planets within the hierarchies of the many local universes.

The Hub: The psychic epicenter of the Web; an autonomous zone of interdimensional possibilities which developed over time and was used by the Helianx to facilitate the creation of localized wormholes.

Architectural worlds: Certain planets within the higher frequencies of the celestial realms are artificially constructed worlds, built to perfectly serve their purposes. All headquarter planets are believed to be artificially constructed.   (*Urantia Book*)

Energy Beings: A general term for the many spirit entities whose area of influence lies in the organization of primal matter.   (*Urantia Book*)

Indwelling Deva: The autonomous organizing principle of all complex biological systems. When an individual of any species attains a harmonious spiritual intelligence, a conscious collaborative relationship with their deva can ensure perfect health and wellbeing.

Experimental planet: On every tenth planet, the Life Carriers are permitted to experiment, to put into practice what they have previously learned in their search for optimum physical vehicles for spiritual beings.   (*Urantia Book*)

Life Carriers: Those celestials entrusted with the development and seeding of organic life on all inhabitable planets.   (*Urantia Book*)

Parthenogenesis: A form of asexual reproduction in which females produce eggs that develop without fertilization from the male sperm. The Helianx used this technique when they needed to build up their numbers rapidly.

Foraminifera: Single-celled animals with chalky shells. Most are marine and the thick calcium sediment on the ocean-floor is partially created by their shells.

Rock Devas: Subsequent to their discovery of the ultimatonic basis of physical matter, the Helianx came to believe that even inanimate matter possessed animating principles, devas, with whom it was possible to communicate.

Nature Spirits: Spirit beings, generally invisible to a planetary population and whose role it is to nurture biological life once it has established itself. Deva can be used as a synonym for Nature Spirit. Mortal beings on all planets can be said to be in-dwelt by a Deva, responsible for the efficient workings of the physical vehicle.

Sirius Star System: A binary star system (claimed by some to be a triune system) at a distance of 8.57 light years from Earth. Believed by the Dogon and Bozo tribes of Mali to have sent extraterrestrial missions to this planet some five thousand years ago and who maintain a kinship with certain cetacean species. *(The Sirius Mystery by Robert Temple)*

Aquatic ape hypothesis: The theory in evolutionary biology that proposes early human ancestors spent periods of time living in semi-aquatic conditions, and is thought to contrast with the Savanna Theory of human origin held by many paleoanthropologists. As is often the case, both theories are likely true. *(The Aquatic Ape by Elaine Morgan)*

Omega-3 fatty acids: Polyunsaturated fatty acids found most abundantly in oily fish. Eight percent of the human brain is comprised of omega-3's, and it is known to have membrane-enhancing capabilities in brain cells. *(Wikipedia)*

Nommo: Collective name of the extraterrestrials from star system Sirius as given to the Dogon of Mali. These ETs maintain they have a direct relationship with Earth's cetaceans and regard humanity as an "interrupted creation". *(The Sirius Mystery by Robert Temple)*

Itibi-Ra: An advanced race of humanoid ETs hailing from two planets, Itibi-Ra 1 and Itibi-Ra 11, in a nearby solar system. Compassionate and epicurean, they visit Earth to cultivate gustatory delicacies while also working as healers amongst humanity's poor and dispossessed. *(UFO Contact from Planet Itibi-Ra by Ludwig F. Pallmann & Wendelle C. Stevens)*

Intraterrestrials: Entities hailing from the inner realms of the celestials, but who are not angels. They were originally mortal beings on material planets who then volunteer for service on primitive worlds. They are given the appropriate material bodies to survive the denser conditions of planetary life. *(Urantia Book--although "intraterrestrial" is the author's term.)*

Local System Headquarters: A Local System of 1000 inhabitable planets is the smallest administrative unit (apart from a single planet) in the Multiverse. A headquarters planet is an architectural sphere in the celestial realms and was the location, in this case, of the celestial rebellion which so profoundly affected Earth and 36 other planets. *(Urantia Book)*

Prince's staff: Whilst the Prince and his assistant are both drawn from a high order of celestials, the 100 staff are merely mortal beings from other planets who have died, progressed through the subsequent levels to the Local System HQ, and who then volunteer to return to a primitive world. *(Urantia Book)*

Midwayers, or Midway Creatures: The direct offspring of the Prince's staff; not subject to death and many of whom were invisible to human eye. Of a total of 50,000, over 40,000 sided with the rebel elements. Although the rebel Midwayers were removed over 2,000 years ago, those remaining loyal to System administration continue to be active on Earth. *(Urantia Book)*

Violet blood: The second of the authorized intraterrestrial interventions into human evolution involves the infusion of a slightly higher frequency genetic endowment which results in more acute senses and less fearful natures.   (*Urantia Book*)

Neanderthals: One of a number of early humanoid races of the Homo genus that inhabited Europe and parts of western Asia from about 230,000 to 29,000 years ago.

Cro-Magnon: Considered the oldest of the anatomically modern humans who flourished from about 35,000 to 10,000 years ago. The subspecies of Homo sapiens believed to have been most positively effected by the genetic infusion of violet blood. They eliminated and replaced the more primitive Neanderthals.   (*Urantia Book*)

Chromatophores: Pigment cells Nöé absorbed from the local cephalopods and arranged along the surface of hir body that sHe could micro-modulate for camouflage or visual display.

Outer Space Levels: Four great bands of matter in very early states of organization that encircle the seven superuniverses from some 400,000 to 50 million light years from the edge of the Grand Universe.   (*Urantia Book*)

Some references have been offered to encourage further research. Definitions of terms derived from the Urantia Book should be regarded as personal to the author and do not necessarily reflect the understanding of others who read this book.

The Gift of the Rainbow Serpent: Mount Tamalpais, Northern California

Timothy Wyllie is the author four books on non-human intelligences. His first book, *Dolphins ETs & Angels*, first published in 1984, remains in print and is considered a classic in its field. *Ask Your Angels*, which he wrote with Alma Daniel and Andrew Ramer has become an international bestseller and has been translated into eight languages to date. *Adventures Among Spiritual Intelligences*, originally published by Bear & Company in 1992 as *Dolphins, Telepathy & Underwater Birthing*, is the second book to investigate how other spiritual intelligences are interacting with our world, and was republished in a new edition in 2001 by Origin Press. *Rising Angels* is the culmination of Timothy's 30 years of interspecies exploration and published by Inner Traditions in 2011.

The Helianx Proposition, which he has been working on since 1979, resulted indirectly from his explorations of other realms of existence. That *The Helianx Proposition* emerged as a fable--a creation myth of sorts--allows the reader to absorb the concepts without having to rationalize away the information coded into the Text.

The Helianx Proposition includes a 30-minute DVD of the author reading the Text at dusk on top of a mesa in the American Southwest, with a superbly animated computer enhancement created by the digital photographer, Flame Schon. The original music was composed and recorded by Jim Wilson and Walker Barnard. Also included in the Collectors Edition are a short animated DVD feature called *The Helianx Awakens*; together with two CDs of spoken word material interwoven with music and which are broadly relevant to the themes in the book.

Working with the New York artist, June Atkin, and by sending drawings back and forth through the mail, Timothy and June are building a series of collaborative graphics exploring the theme of the emergent female principle.

Two CDs of spoken word material under the general title of *The Path of the Rainbow Serpent* with music composed by Emmy Award winner Jim Wilson is included with the limited editions that are available on request from the author..

Timothy was born and raised in England and was trained as an architect in London before having a hand in co-founding a spiritual community and moving to America in the late 1960s. He now lives in a house of his own creation in the high desert of New Mexico. He is currently continuing to draw his graphics and is working on the next books in the *Adventures Among Spiritual Intelligences* series.

For more information on the books, artwork, music and poetry of Timothy Wyllie, please visit his website. www.timothywyllie.com